VIRAGO
MODERN CLASSICS
642

Joan Aiken (1924–2004) was born in Rye, Sussex. She was the daughter of the American poet Conrad Aiken, and her step-father was English writer Martin Armstrong. For both Joan and her sister, novelist Jane Aiken Hodge, writing was in their blood.

Joan Aiken wrote over a hundred books and is recognised as one of the classic children's authors of the twentieth century. Amanda Craig, in *The Times*, wrote, 'She was a consummate story-teller, one that each generation discovers anew', and Philip Pullman said, 'Joan Aiken's invention seemed inexhaustible, her high spirits a blessing, her sheer story-telling zest a phenomenon. She was a literary treasure, and her books will continue to delight for many years to come.'

She wrote her first novel, *The Kingdom and the Cave*, when she was just seventeen years old, and the story collection *The Serial Garden*, featuring the magical Armitage family, spans her entire writing career, from her earliest published short story, 'Yes, But Today is Tuesday' to the stories she wrote at the end of her life. Her best-known books are *The Wolves of Willoughby Chase* chronicles and the *Arabel's Raven* series. Joan Aiken received the Edgar Allan Poe Award in the United States as well as the Guardian Award for Fiction. She was decorated with an MBE for her services to children's books.

The Kingdom and the Cave

JOAN AIKEN

Illustrated by Peter Bailey

virago

VIRAGO

This edition published in Great Britain in 2015 by Virago Press

1 3 5 7 9 10 8 6 4 2

First published in Great Britain in 1960 by Abelard-Schuman Limited

A CIP catalogue record for this book
is available from the British Library.

ISBN 978-0-349-00587-4

Typeset in Goudy by M Rules
Printed and bound in Great Britain by
Clays Ltd, St Ives plc

Papers used by Virago are from well-managed forests
and other responsible sources.

MIX
Paper from
responsible sources
FSC
www.fsc.org   FSC® C104740

Virago
An imprint of
Little, Brown Book Group
Carmelite House
50 Victoria Embankment
London EC4Y 0DZ

An Hachette UK Company
www.hachette.co.uk

www.virago.co.uk

The Kingdom
and the Cave

1

Mickle had lived in the Royal Palace of Astalon for some years before things began to go wrong.

Officially, Mickle was the Court Cat; principally, he was the dear friend and companion of the Crown Prince Michael, who thought he knew everything there was to be known about the cat. Actually he knew next to nothing, as we shall see.

Mickle was greatly respected by everyone, and had a most comfortable life. On the whole he preferred to catch his own meals in the Palace grounds, for he was a strong and stealthy hunter, but if ever he condescended to visit the kitchens, there would be a royal meal for him of game and fish from the King's table, and a bowl of fresh milk was always standing in his own room near the foot of the grand staircase.

In here there was always a fire burning, with a cushion in

front of it. The walls were decorated with a frieze of the most delectable animals, birds flying, and fish leaping from their streams. A mechanical stroker occupied one corner. Mickle had only to lie on a pleasantly rough and prickly mat and an automatic hand would stroke him, scratching under his chin and gently rubbing his ears.

He had another bed in the garden, in case he took a fancy to spend the night out: a windproof box lined with hay where he could lie and watch the stars, or listen to the rain. But most often he would climb up and spend the night curled under a corner of Prince Michael's eiderdown. They had come to an amicable arrangement that Mickle had three-quarters of the bed and the Prince the rest. The only person who objected was the Head Nursery Maid who found muddy cat-footprints on the cloth-of-silver sheets. But at the time this story begins she had resigned long ago, and her place had been taken by a governess, Miss Simkin.

One autumn day Mickle, who had been taking a dust bath in his private flowerbed, among the micklemouse daisies, decided that it was a long time since he had visited his friend Minerva, the old mare who lived in the field beyond the Palace garden.

Minerva was cropping steadily, head down, on the autumn grass. Mickle seated himself on a gatepost and watched gravely for some time. Then she moved over slowly, taking a mouthful or two on her way, more from absent-mindedness than hunger.

'Well, Mickle,' she said, when she was within speaking distance, 'it's some time since you've been this way. How's the family?'

'That's what I've come to talk about,' replied Mickle. 'Listen – but look as if you were eating grass and weren't very interested. I'm beginning to distrust everyone these days.'

Minerva dropped her head among the dry grass at the foot of the fence and snuffled disgustedly.

'Well – go on?'

'I'm getting worried,' Mickle confessed. 'I don't like the look of things at all. The King spends hours and hours every day shut up in the library, doing secret experiments. I think it's some kind of magic – he often has a strong smell of magic about him when he comes out.'

Minerva nodded. 'All that family are the same,' she said. 'His father was, *and* the Old King before him too, so I'm told. They're all mad on experimenting and trying to find things out by magic, and the trouble is they seem to be no good at it.'

'It's some invention of the Old King's that he's trying to rediscover now,' Mickle told her. 'I heard him talking to the Queen one day at breakfast.

'"Must you go and work in the library today?" I heard her

say. "I must," he answered. "I'm nearly finished, I hope. Think how important it will be when I've found it." "Well," she said, "and in the meantime suppose the Kingdom's invaded by the Under People—?" Then the King looked round, as if he expected to see people hiding behind the door, and said to the Queen, "Don't you see, once we have the magic box we shall be safe even if they do come. The Old King told his son, my father, when he was a boy, that it would save the country in its darkest hour."

'Then somebody came in and they stopped talking.'

'Well,' said Minerva, 'that sounds pretty sinister, I must say. I wonder what this box is? And where does Prince Michael come into all this?'

'I don't think he knows about it,' said Mickle. 'Such a lot of the time nowadays he's being taught Latin and algebra by that governess. I don't think he's noticed anything wrong. He seems fairly cheerful.'

Minerva thought for some time, breathing about in the grass. Then she said,

'It seems to me that you'd better find out some more about what the King does in the library. We want to know about this magic box, what it is and where it is. Why can't he find it? And I wonder who the Under People are? I don't like the sound of them. See what you can find out, and we'll discuss what to do.'

'That's a good idea,' said Mickle, much relieved at having

another opinion. 'Not that it's very easy to find out what's going on in the library. The King's had all the furniture cleared out except a big table and a locked cupboard, so there's nowhere to hide, and he always locks the door when he comes out.'

'Can't you climb in through the window?'

'I could try,' Mickle said doubtfully.

'Well I leave it to you,' Minerva grunted. 'I know nothing about getting into windows or hiding in rooms. If people lived in fields, sensibly, they wouldn't have these difficulties.' And she moved away and began to crop in good earnest.

Mickle jumped down and stalked off towards the Palace. Dusk, and a thin rain, was beginning to fall. He made his way, by means of a trellis, a balcony, and a waterpipe, on to the roof, cursing under his breath at the slippery tiles. The library window was in a gable at the end of the Palace. Mickle perched on the peak of the gable, looking down at the narrow wet sill which he had to reach.

'What's needed here isn't a cat, it's a monkey,' he grumbled to himself. 'Heaven knows why I let myself be persuaded into it.'

He waited ten minutes till it was quite dark, and then edged his way down the side of the roof until he came to the best jumping-off place. He balanced, rocked himself on clustered paws, and jumped neatly across. He had calculated to land in the middle of the sill, but there was an eighth of an

5

inch of water on it and he slid perilously near the edge. He recovered his balance and turned. The window was open. Inside everything was as dark as pitch, so he decided to take a risk and slipped in as quietly as the shadow of a bat on a moonless night. It was really black inside; although Mickle was a cat he couldn't see a thing, but he remembered the layout of the room and glided across to the cupboard. He sat down beside it and stayed perfectly still for half an hour, for he knew that the essence of good spying is not to be in a hurry.

He was just deciding that it was safe to move when a sound made him freeze. It was one brief footstep and a click, followed by a rapid buzzing, which puzzled him. He could have sworn there was not a soul there except himself. What was making the noise? He sat tight and waited.

In a moment there was another click, and a shaft of light suddenly shone across the room, nearly scaring Mickle out of his skin. It came from a tiny pinpoint halfway up the wall to his right, widened into a broad ray, and lit up a white square on the opposite wall.

The ray remained steady for a minute, then it changed and wavered, and a picture took shape in the white square. A long procession of cloaked men and horses was moving down a slope. The horses were carrying loads, and the men were leading them. They stopped in a group at the bottom of the steep path, among some dark yew-trees, and the men unloaded the bundles and carried them through the trees. Then Mickle could see the mouth of a cave in the high, ivy-grown bank, which was almost a cliff; there seemed to be a waterfall nearby, because beyond some rocks a cloud of spray continually rose, and spouts of water ran down the face of the bank and over the cave mouth. A stream came out of the cave and the men waded along it in single file and disappeared inside.

Then the picture changed, and Mickle saw them sludging along inside. They turned into a smaller cave and unfastened their bundles. Mickle saw great jewels, and carved chests of gold pieces, and three crowns, and a massive sceptre of gold with a ruby blazing at one end. There was a small carved metal box, too, which they seemed to treat with particular care. They stacked all these things on a shelf of rock, and then went swiftly out, the way they had come.

The cave remained empty, and the picture flickered and grew dim for a while. Then it cleared again to show the same cave. Mickle supposed that some time had gone by. More men appeared, carrying weapons and baskets and chests. Their clothes were quite different from those of the first lot, and there were women with them, in long cloaks. When they saw the treasure they seemed highly excited and all clapped their hands and waved their arms, with their mouths open as if they were shouting. Immediately the picture became dark, and stayed so for some time.

Mickle grew bored and wondered if that was the end. Somebody else apparently shared his feelings, for he heard a soft voice from beyond the ray whisper,

'I don't think much of the King's magic. We haven't found out anything we don't know yet.'

'Don't be a fool,' said another voice. 'And keep quiet. We want to find out what *he* knows.'

Mickle was startled. He had thought there was no one there, he could see no one, and evidently they could not see him, but it was plain that at least two other people were in the room with him, and, what was more, he was fairly sure they had no right to be there. Mickle began to think it was not at all a good thing for them to be seeing the King's pictures, which were obviously important and secret. He stole sideways towards the ray, and saw that it came out of a little box set on a tripod. There seemed only one thing to do, so he upset the tripod and brought the box crashing to the floor.

Immediately there was dead silence. The room was like black velvet. Mickle backed away to the window, even more silently than he had come in. He kept every whisker separate in case they might brush together and betray him.

Then he heard soft footsteps which moved this way and that, and finally came towards him. Mickle waited no longer. He sprang on to the windowsill and recklessly jumped out into the darkness.

2

On the morning after Mickle's adventure in the library the King seemed very worried about something, and as soon as James the footman had brought in the breakfast kidneys and mushrooms and gone out again, he jumped up, shut the door, and came back to the table with his hands in his pockets.

'Well?' the Queen asked. She was reading the last paragraph of a letter from her sister. 'Isabella says the children are all well. They send their love ... Well, how did it go off?'

'Something terrible has happened!' said the King. 'When I got up there after that wretched banquet, someone had been in the library. The apparatus was upset, it had evidently been used by someone else and then broken.'

'So you don't know anything more?'

'I don't know, and what's worse, some enemy does.'

'Well,' thought Mickle under the table, 'if they don't

know more than I do, they know precious little.' He stretched with satisfaction, though he was uncommonly stiff and scratched from the rose-bushes into which he had fallen.

'What are you going to do?' the Queen asked. She seemed irritable this morning. 'Eat your breakfast before it's cold, for goodness' sake.'

The King sat down and began absently eating his kidneys.

'I've set a spell working to find out who was in there last night.'

'And what good will that do?' said the Queen. 'You've a pretty good idea, anyway, haven't you?' The King admitted, shuddering, that he had.

Then Prince Michael came in, extremely late for breakfast, and no more was said. The King rolled up his napkin and walked towards the door.

'Are you going to the library?' asked the Queen sharply.

'I was.'

'Well, you can't go yet. The Pomeranian Ambassador is coming at eleven, and it's most important that you should see him. We can't afford to offend anybody just now. *Michael!* You can't eat a piece as big as that. Cut it in half.'

'My goodness,' thought Mickle, 'she *is* in a temper this morning.'

He wondered what he ought to do. He might consult

Minerva, but perhaps it would be better to wait and find out what the King's spell said – it might tell who the other watchers had been. Could they be Under People? He made up his mind to try and follow the King into the library, but evidently that would not be until after the audience with the Pomeranian Ambassador.

A nice rest in the sun, thought Mickle, would be a good thing for his stiffness. He was moving unobtrusively towards the door when Queen Elfrida caught sight of him.

'My goodness!' she exclaimed, 'What ever is the matter with that cat? He looks as if he'd been dragged backwards through a raspberry hedge. James, take him out and give him a wash and brush.'

Mickle did not manage to get away from James before he had been thoroughly washed, until his coat felt stiff and soapy, and then combed till he was sore all over. He was a well-bred cat and did not try to scratch James, though he murmured some unrepeatable things about the Queen. When it was over he took himself off to his room and washed himself again, from head to foot. Then he lay down under the mechanical stroker and was smoothed and patted and pummelled until he felt respectable again, and fit to appear with proper dignity as Court Cat. He stalked out magnificently through the hall and into the Throne Room, where the audience was in full swing.

The Pomeranian Ambassador was a fat little man, dressed

very elegantly. He nodded his head a number of times, and said a great many flattering things about the Kingdom of Astalon, but not as if he meant them. The King appeared terribly bored and preoccupied. He kept glancing nervously towards the Throne Room clock. Once he caught the Queen's eye and looked guilty.

Mickle soon decided that the affair was very stupid and not worth his attention, and he curled up on a scarlet cushion and went to sleep, just keeping the slit of one eye open. After three-quarters of an hour of polite and boring talk the Ambassador departed. The King jumped up in relief. Immediately Mickle was wide awake and sliding along behind him as he left the room.

Luckily the King had on ceremonial dress which included a long flowing train; Mickle concealed himself very successfully behind this as it swept about, and followed upstairs to the library. He had to scurry round behind the King as he turned to shut the door, and then thought he would be discovered, for the King took his great cloak off and hung it on a chair. It proved a blessing, however, for Mickle was able to hide underneath it.

The King unlocked the cupboard, and Mickle nearly got a crick in his neck trying to see what was inside. He had a glimpse of strange apparatus – glass flasks, and long wands, and a skull, and gallipots, and a lot of thick, musty-looking books. The smell of magic came very strongly out of this cupboard.

The King carried a flat black box over to the table. It had a handle at one side and a long tube coiled up on top. When he poured some red liquid into the tube and wound the handle, the machine began to buzz. After a minute it said, 'Speak.'

'Did you listen in this room?' said the King.

'Yes.'

'What did you hear?'

Then to Mickle's surprise the machine repeated the conversation held by the two soft voices the night before.

'Thank goodness I didn't speak,' he thought. 'I'll remember that contrivance in future when I go spying.'

'H'm,' the King muttered to himself. 'Luckily it looks as if they weren't very satisfied either. I wonder what upset them? I suppose they have enemies of their own who put a spoke in their wheel. Well they don't know now, and I don't know, so I shall just have to start the work over again.' He turned once more to the box.

'Who were those voices?' he asked it.

'Those from Down Under.'

'Did they learn what I want to know?'

'They learned, and they did not learn.'

'Shall I find out the secret?'

'No. Others will find it out before you.'

The King seemed much put out by this, and walked about the room for some time before he asked the next question.

'Will they invade my country, or shall I invade them?'

'Your son will go alone among them, but they will come into your country in thousands.'

At this the King became very pale and shut down the machine with a click. Mickle heard him muttering, 'Oh, goodness me. Why did I ever take to meddling with magic? It doesn't do any good to know the future – it only upsets you. What *shall* I do now? I can't possibly tell Elfrida.'

He walked out of the room with his shoulders hunched and his head drooping. He was so upset that he didn't even put on his cloak or shut the door.

Mickle waited till he was safely away, and then began to explore. He could get nothing further out of the talking machine, but to his joy the King had left the cupboard unlocked. He hated the strong smell of magic that breathed out at him, nearly choking him and making his whiskers vibrate in a most uncomfortable way, but in a minute these effects wore off, and he began to feel lively and exhilarated.

He made a tremendous effort, and jumped up on to the top shelf, alighting gently beside the skull. This shelf was full of glass vessels, most of them with very strange shapes. Mickle had not the least idea what they were used for, and moved down to the next shelf. Here there were books: 'The Amateur Magician', 'Spell-making for Beginners', 'Teach Yourself the Black Arts', and so on. Mickle wasted no time here, either.

He moved on to the next shelf where there was a lot of miscellaneous clutter: little bottles and phials, pillboxes marked 'Cat Ointment' – Mickle looked askance at this – little pestles and mortars and blowpipes and magic scissors. Mickle guessed that most of these were pretty trumpery devices, the sort of things that real magicians would despise, probably obtained through the mail-order columns of the 'Necromancer's Weekly'. Some of the things looked as if they would break at a touch. The magic scissors were already bent.

'The King's no use at anything,' he thought pityingly.

But he did take out a red leather collar attached to a card marked 'Magic Collar, Cats, for use of. Three wishes twelve-hourly', thinking that it might come in handy. It fastened itself round his neck.

There were some jottings on sheets of paper in the King's handwriting which he studied. They were headed 'Notes on the Under People', and consisted of scattered sentences, hurriedly scrawled as if the King had written them down while listening to the magic gramophone.

'They live in a huge cave. They are thought to be boring upwards. Giant worms and flying ants. Underground magic. Secret treasure kept in rock chamber – could this be Old King's treasure? Have they got the box?'

Underneath in a clearer handwriting the King had added, 'How did they get there? How many are there? How about sending spies down there? (difficult). Where can one get in?'

Mickle had read this far when he heard the King's step, slow and dragging, outside the door. He looked about frantically for cover.

'My goodness, I wish I were out of here and in Minerva's field,' he thought despairingly. 'The King will be sure to think I'm a spy.'

Instantly everything went hazy and rocked around him; then he was sitting on a tussock of grass and Minerva was looking at him in an unfriendly way.

'I don't know what you think you're doing,' she remarked irritably. 'Gone one minute and here the next. Personally I think it's in bad taste not to give decent notice when you call on a person. I don't like this sort of thing, not at my age, and so I'll thank you to remember.'

Mickle explained that it must have been the magic collar, cats, for use of, and apologized a good deal before the old horse was mollified. Then she said, 'Well and good – but the next time you do it, don't pop up under my nose. Now, what have you learned?'

Mickle told her all that he had seen and heard, and she reflected in silence for a while.

'We don't seem to have advanced very far,' she said. 'We still don't know what the secret of that box is, nor *where* it is, nor much about the Under People, except that they live in a cave.'

'*Those from Down Under*,' murmured Mickle. 'Do you

suppose they were the people in the picture, the ones who put the treasure in the cave, or the ones who found it? Still there weren't thousands of them, and that gadget of the King's said distinctly, "They will come into your country in their thousands."' He sat brooding, while Minerva tried to fan her head with her tail.

Presently he said, 'Last winter I was sitting outside a mousehole in the Palace cellars when I heard some mice talking. Well you know, as a rule mice talk pretty fair twaddle, but this seemed different. One of them said, "We think somebody lives down there because we've heard banging. Several mice have been down to see but they never come back." I didn't think much of it at the time, because they might have meant anything from rabbits to badgers, but now I'm not so sure.'

'Now I come to think of it,' said Minerva, 'I've heard odd rumbling noises underground.'

'I'll get hold of my friend Brock the badger over at Dingle Warren and find out if he has any views,' suggested Mickle. 'He ought to know about underground things if anyone does. Now, about the King's box. Do you think that could be among the treasure I saw? There *was* a box.'

'I seem to remember,' said Minerva, 'my father telling us something about some royal treasure – the crown jewels I think it was – being stolen many years ago and never found. I wonder if it could be that?'

'Who stole it?'

But Minerva, most annoyingly, could not remember any more, and her father was dead. However she had a very old great-uncle still alive, and she thought he might remember. He was a weight-carrying hunter, pensioned off now these many years, living over near Thraun.

'You'll have to go and see him then,' said Mickle impatiently. 'Could you go tonight? It's no use my calling on Brock tonight, because I happen to know he's arranged a hunting expedition. I'll come to Thraun with you.'

Minerva grumbled and said that her rheumatism was terribly bad, but when Mickle suggested using his magic collar she flatly declared that nothing would persuade her to use such a contraption; she was still capable of trotting a few miles on a fine night.

'One last thing,' she said, 'it looks as if young Prince Michael is going to be mixed up in all this, from what the talking machine said. I think he had better be warned, and told what we know. It may be useful to have a human ally.'

'Yes, I think you're right,' Mickle agreed, 'the time has come; though he'll be a bit of a responsibility. Michael's a good sort – he's got plenty of sense, considering what fools his parents are – but these humans are so inefficient; they can never take care of themselves.'

He trotted off with his tail waving.

3

'*Amnis, axis, caulis, collis,*' muttered Prince Michael to himself. 'Drat this thing, I shall never know it. *Clunis, crinis, fascis, follis.*' His eyes strayed away from his Latin grammar. Through the window he could see his mother being polite to the Pomeranian Ambassador in the rose garden. The King was lying down with a headache; he had looked dreadfully ill at lunch and had gone off soon afterwards. Miss Simkin, the governess, was out for the afternoon. The whole Palace seemed to be deserted. He gave a great yawn and turned back to his Latin.

'*Amnis, axis, caulis, collis.*' But it would not stick, and he became more and more bored. Nothing interesting ever happens now, he thought. I learn a lot of stuff with Miss Simkin that does me no good, and no one nice ever comes to stay, and Father and Mother always seem to be out of sorts. Even Mickle's away more often than not.

Just at that moment he heard a peremptory mew outside the schoolroom door. He opened it. There was Mickle.

'Prtnyow?' said Mickle again, and walked a little way off with his head turned, plainly inviting Michael to follow him. Michael willingly dropped the Latin grammar and went with him along the corridor, down the grand staircase, out across the lawns behind the Palace, and through the massive rhododendron shrubbery.

'Wherever are you taking me, Mickle?' exclaimed the Prince.

Mickle only went faster. They passed into an orchard and crossed it. In a far corner, standing by itself, was a huge old walnut tree. It had once been a much-visited castle of Michael's, before Miss Simkin used up such a lot of his time. He had driven large iron staples into the trunk, to be used as steps, and nailed a board platform across the high fork. It made a lovely place to lie and read, with a cupboard underneath.

Michael went hand-over-hand up the steps, and Mickle waited until he was settled in the fork and then scurried up the trunk, scorning the help of the staples. Michael was lying at full length with his head on a pile of sacking, staring through half-closed eyes at the bright afternoon sky.

'Now then,' said Mickle, 'I want you to pay close attention to what I am going to say, please.'

The Prince was so astonished that he nearly rolled off the platform.

'When did you learn to talk?' he exclaimed.

'Pooh,' said Mickle. 'I've always been able to talk your language. There's nothing to it. Now if it were a question of the Universal Animal Language, in which, as well as having to know what every sound means, you have to learn the precise significance of every twist of a whisker or the way a horse lays its ears back or a fish wriggles, then I should expect a little surprise.'

'And do you speak that?' asked Michael.

'Naturally,' said Mickle. 'You'll have to learn some of it yourself. But that isn't the point. I brought you here to tell you something extremely important and private.'

'If you can talk,' persisted Michael, 'why haven't you ever talked to me before?'

Mickle gave him a withering look. 'I could see how it would be,' he remarked. 'Why, if I'd told you when you were any younger you would have plagued the life out of me every day with stupid questions like that one. All cats can talk, but none of them choose to let on they can. Let the poor silly humans get into their own messes, we'll keep clear of them, is our motto.'

'Well then, what did you bring me here to tell me?' asked Michael humbly.

'*Now* you're talking,' said the cat. 'And for goodness' sake listen carefully. You'll find it quite hard enough to follow without looking at swallows the whole time.' Michael shifted his eyes guiltily.

'Minerva and I,' Mickle went on, 'have discovered that there's a plot. Your father is searching for something – a magic box, we think – and some enemies are looking for it, too. We suspect they are Underground People. They appear to be numerous and powerful, and may be going to invade the Kingdom, and it's our duty to stop them, as your father seems to have more or less given up hope.'

Michael's eyes shone with interest, but he controlled himself by a great effort and did not ask questions. Mickle went on:

'Minerva and I are going to Thraun tonight to visit a great-uncle of hers who may know about some treasure that was once lost. We think the magic box was with it. As I find it rather inconvenient riding on Minerva's back, I thought it would be a good thing if you came too, and then you can ride her and carry me.'

'Yes,' said Michael breathlessly.

'So you'd better meet me by the waxberry bush at the kitchen-garden gate at ten o'clock tonight.'

'How will you know the time?'

'Cats always know the time,' said Mickle, stretching. He dropped over the edge of the platform with a flick of his tail. Next moment he suddenly and silently returned.

'It occurs to me,' he said, dusting a cobweb out of his whiskers, 'that you'd be less of a handicap if you started to learn the Universal Animal Language at once. Of course it's not necessary for you to understand rare creatures like sunfish, or blue-snouted mandrills, but there's no harm in your beginning to pick up a few of the commoner bird and animal signs.'

'Are you going to teach me?' asked Michael apprehensively. Though he was devoted to Mickle, he suspected the cat would be an even more exacting teacher than Miss Simkin.

'Gracious, no,' said Mickle. 'I haven't the time to waste. No, a friend of mine is going to teach you. He's waiting down below because he's getting a bit old and doesn't care for climbing.'

'What is your friend's name?' the Prince asked as he scrambled down.

'Professor Nicodemus.'

That suggested little to Michael. 'Is he a cat?' he asked.

'Well – no,' said Mickle in slight embarrassment, 'as a matter of fact he's a water rat, but of course a most unusual water rat, very cultured, or I wouldn't know him. The Professor did me a great kindness once. Maybe some time he'll tell you about it. He speaks a little English. You ought to know the rudiments of the Universal Language by this evening, if you work hard. Ah, here he is. Don't tread on him. Professor, this is Prince Michael. He's not as foolish as the run of them, and I know I'm leaving him in good hands. Now I must dash.' And he was off in a whisk, through the long grass, leaving master and pupil gazing at each other. Michael respectfully picked up the little beady-eyed brown creature.

'How do you do?' he said shyly.

A tiny squeak answered him. He bent down his ear and listened.

'If you weesh to spee-eek to me, you must spee-eek very high, no?' said Professor Nicodemus shrilly in his ear. 'I cannot hear your so low mutter.'

'How do you do?' squeaked Michael up in the top of his head.

'Ah, so! I see you make a very quee-eek pupil. Now take me somewhere quiet and I begin to tee-eech you.'

Michael thought the schoolroom would be as good a place as any, for Miss Simkin would not be back till late. He carried the Professor carefully in a large leaf and made his way there without meeting anyone.

Then the lesson began. The Professor carefully explained the basic signs and noises of the Universal Language – very simple ones, all of these, like 'Go away', and 'I am hungry', and 'Please direct me to the nearest pond'. He made Michael repeat them again and again.

Then Michael learned the principal signs used by each individual animal – the way squirrels tell each other about rotten branches, the special signs birds have about nests, and so on. The time passed quickly, and soon Michael had to hustle the Professor into the drawer he kept his fossils in while James the footman brought in tea. He was having it by himself today, as the Pomeranian Ambassador was being entertained at a tea party by the Queen.

'Would you like some milk, or a piece of cake?' asked Michael as the door shut behind James.

'Ah yes. Some mee-eelk if you plee-eese. I am hoarse with squeaking so low,' said the Professor, reappearing.

'I feel a bit sore myself,' squeaked Michael feelingly, and by mutual consent they rested their voices until the end of tea. Afterwards the lesson went on, and Michael began to feel that he was getting quite a grasp of the language. He was able to lean out of the window and say, 'Have you seen the eggs of my aunt?' to a passing starling.

'Not bad,' said the Professor. 'When I shall have taught you a few days you will know all the commoner bee-eests. I shall stay with you till then – no?'

Michael said he would be delighted, and made the Professor a comfortable nest in a little box lined with hay.

'I wish Latin had as much sense in it as this language,' he thought, as the Professor curled up for a much-needed sleep, and he picked up the Latin grammar and began again on his homework. But he found it harder than ever to concentrate, and when Miss Simkin presently came in and demanded to hear *Amnis, axis*, it went very haltingly though he could have showed her exactly how a horse blows out its nostrils when it is saying 'Look at that horrible train.'

Miss Simkin stayed to read aloud to him while he ate his supper. This was annoying, because he wanted to give some cheese to the Professor, but at last he managed to slip a good large piece into his pocket while she was turning a page.

He went to bed as early as he could. The Professor had declined to come on the Thraun expedition as he was getting old and the jolting was bad for his gout. Miss Simkin said good night and went off to her own room at the other end of the Palace. Michael knew the King and Queen were not likely to come in, on account of a banquet for the Ambassador.

With a beating heart, he arranged bolsters in the bed to look like himself and Mickle to the casual eye, and then climbed out of his window into a pear tree – a convenient route he often used – and slipped round to the waxberry bush by the garden gate. For a terrible minute he thought he was too late and no one was there, but no: the bush parted and a black velvet shape rubbed against his ankle.

4

Minerva was asleep, squarely planted on her four legs. They made their way to her quietly and Michael touched her on the shoulder. Instantly she woke up, swinging her head slowly and inquiringly around.

'Oh it's you, is it?'

Mickle sniffed. 'You're a nice one. If the plan had depended on you we shouldn't have got far tonight.'

'Yes, but it didn't,' Minerva answered placidly. 'Good evening, Michael.'

'Good evening,' Michael said. He was relieved to find that the language spoken by the horse and cat was a good deal easier to understand than when it was reproduced in the Professor's squeaky tones.

'Well,' said the old horse resignedly, 'I suppose you want to get on my back.'

Here there was a slight difficulty. Michael could not

29

mount on her bare back while he was holding the cat, and Minerva flatly refused to let Mickle jump on to her. 'I *know* you'll stick your claws in me,' she insisted. So Mickle perched on a gatepost while Michael vaulted on, and then it was easy enough to lean sideways and pick up the cat. Minerva remarked that together they weighed a ton, but this was only to make conversation. They trotted off, throwing enormous shadows in the light of the rising moon.

The way at first lay uphill, but presently they were on a ridge, and Minerva broke into a rapid swinging canter. Michael had slight difficulty in balancing, without bridle or stirrups, and with a large and dignified cat impeding him.

It was a glorious ride, though. They could not see the country below, because a great white mist like the sea was crawling and creeping across it, but ahead of them hill after hill lay bare and silver in the moonlight. Minerva was not nearly so aged and rheumaticky as she liked to make out; she kept on at her steady canter, eating up the miles, and at about midnight they came to Thraun Head.

'My uncle lives in a field somewhere below here,' said Minerva staring down into the mist. She whinnied shrilly, and far down another whinny answered.

'I'm going to walk down,' said Michael, looking dubiously at the steep slope. 'Shall I carry you, Mickle?'

'I'll go on foot, thanks,' said the cat, and vanished down

the hillside at a gallop. Minerva and the Prince went more carefully, slithering on the short turf, until at the bottom they found Mickle talking politely to a suspicious old brown horse.

'Gracious me, it *is* you, then, Minerva,' he said. 'I wasn't quite sure whether this person was an impostor or not.'

'I've come to ask you for some information,' said Minerva, 'but let's find somewhere less draughty to talk.'

'Are you cold?' her great-uncle asked fussily. 'We can stand in the lee of that shed, and perhaps the child would have the sense to rub you down with a handful of hay.'

They moved round to the sheltered side of the barn. Michael went into the musty darkness inside and felt about for hay. A rat scuttled over his foot, and Michael had the pleasure of squeaking, 'I beg your pardon.'

'Pray don't mention it,' a rather astonished squeak answered him. 'Can I help you?'

'I was looking for a little hay.'

'You'll find a heap about six feet away from your right foot.'

Michael took a big handful and thanked the rat politely.

'What a long time you've been,' said Mickle. 'Poor Minerva is catching her death.'

'So you see,' Minerva was saying earnestly to her great-uncle, 'we want to know who stole the Crown Jewels, and what happened to them.'

'Well,' the uncle replied, 'my grandfather used to tell us a story about treasure when we were young.

'When my grandfather was a colt – and that's going back a good way – there was a Lord Roger Wyburn who owned all the land round here. Folks used to say he was the wickedest man in Astalon – the wickedest and the wealthiest. But wickedness and wealth didn't content him, he was everlastingly scheming to get more wealth and more power.

'One winter my grandfather got friendly with a dog, Royal, who lived up at Thraun Great House. This dog was a gossip, and many's the bit of news he used to bring out. One bitter evening he told my grandpa that there were funny doings up at the Great House. A whole pack of foreigners had come to stay, not Astalon men, but an ugly-looking crew who seemed to be plotting some devilment with Lord Roger and his son – did I tell you his son Giles was even wickeder? And presently Royal discovered that these foreigners and Lord Roger were going to steal the King's jewels out of his Palace, and start a revolution to make Lord Roger King of Astalon. The people didn't care for the king they had then – he was always reading and inventing things, and they never saw him. Now Lord Roger, he was wicked, but he was what you'd call a public man – always riding about the country with lances and scarlet cloaks, and the people liked it and used to cheer him. So he reckoned that if he had plenty of treasure to persuade them with, there wouldn't be any trouble.

'My grandpa never found out how the treasure was stolen from the Palace, but three nights later Lord Roger's horses were taken over the hills to the Royal Park and there the foreigners, all in black cloaks, came sneaking out with great heavy bundles and loaded them up, and they were led away, secret and silent, a long, slow journey, to a place where there were two lakes, one below and one above, with a bridge between them and a waterfall under the bridge. The horses were led down a steep path beside the fall to a dark place with a lot of yew-trees, and there they were tethered while the men took the bundles and hid them somewhere – my grandfather didn't see where.

'Afterwards they went home again, but when they reached Thraun Great House, just at sunrise, some of the King's men burst out of the trees. There was a battle, and Lord Roger was killed, but Giles and the foreigners escaped. The King had discovered the theft, you see, but too late.'

The old horse paused. Michael, who had been vigorously rubbing Minerva with the hay, asked, 'But what happened to the treasure? Didn't the King ever get it back?'

'No, he never found out where they'd hidden it.'

'It was in a cave near the waterfall – or under it,' said Mickle. 'If only we knew where that was. We might try asking some of the birds.'

33

'I don't hold with birds,' Minerva snorted.

'We ought to be off, Minerva, or we won't be home by sunrise,' Mickle said. 'Look at the sky.'

Michael produced biscuits and sugar, and the four of them ate a hasty, standing-up picnic.

'Thank you for your story, old sir,' said Mickle to Minerva's great-uncle. 'At least it shows us we're working on the right lines.'

The old horse nodded politely, stifling a yawn.

'Oh bother,' said Michael. 'How shall we mount? I'll have to lift you on first, Mickle, – *don't* hold on with your claws – and Minerva, you stand very still so that he won't be tempted.'

'And you get on a bit more gently this time, less as if you were pole-vaulting and I was the pole,' said Minerva tartly.

Michael lifted the cat on to Minerva's rump and tried to vault on as carefully as if she were standing on eggs. It was fairly successful, though Mickle grunted as he slid on Minerva's slippery hide. They said goodnight and started the long ride home.

Just before daybreak they arrived at Minerva's paddock. She blew at them by way of goodbye and went straight off to sleep where she stood. The other two crept quietly across the garden and climbed up to Michael's window. Mickle jumped straight on to the bed and snuggled himself a nest in the eiderdown. By the time the Prince had undressed he was asleep, and taking up nine-tenths of the bed.

5

Mickle was lying in front of the schoolroom fire, smiling to himself and licking first one paw and then another in a leisurely way. The Prince was curled up in the window-seat frowning furiously over his Latin grammar or looking out unseeingly over the rainswept garden, muttering, '*Amnis, axis, caulis, collis.*'

And the Professor was curled up snugly in his little box, but nobody saw *him*.

Lessons began at nine. At ten minutes to nine Michael was roused by a hoarse squeak in his ear.

'Pardon me if I interrupt you, but may I make a small requeest?'

'Of course, Professor,' Michael said. 'Can I get you a drink? You sound terribly hoarse.'

'Ah! That ees eet! I thee-eenk I have a queensy.'

'Quinsy?' said Michael. 'Would you like a cough drop?' He

went away and found a little box of them. The Professor opened his mouth to its fullest extent, and Michael rather gingerly popped a gummy cough drop inside. The Professor shut his mouth, and Michael turned his attention to Latin again.

But in a minute he heard an anguished squeak close to his ear. The Professor was standing on his shoulder swishing his tail from side to side with a frantic expression on his face.

'What's the matter?' exclaimed Michael in alarm.

'Eheem goghee heem!' squeaked the Professor unintelligibly.

'Mickle, come and look at the Professor. There's something wrong with him!'

'If you ask me,' said Mickle, looking at him critically, 'he's got that cough drop of yours stuck in his throat. I thought it was a bit big.'

The Professor nodded violently, tried to open his mouth, and failed.

'You'd better squeeze very gently at the sides of his mouth,' Mickle advised. The Prince pressed cautiously on the Professor's whiskered cheeks with finger and thumb. A muffled squeak came out, and Nicodemus lashed his tail madly.

'Shouldn't we prise his mouth open?' Michael asked doubtfully.

'No, you might hurt him. Keep on.'

Michael pressed again, feeling as if he were trying to pop a snapdragon. Then suddenly, with rather the same kind of soft plop, the Professor's jaws came apart, showing the cough drop stuck on his lower teeth. He gave a little gasp of relief and began trying to dislodge it by moving his jaws from side to side.

'Don't do that,' exclaimed Michael, 'you'll get stuck again.'

Miss Simkin came in.

'Put away those things, Michael' – she looked vaguely and short-sightedly at the Professor's box and breakfast dishes – 'and come to the table. It's algebra first today.'

Michael was horrified. At least the Professor wasn't breathless and choking now, but he couldn't be left with his mouth blocked by a huge cough drop. He sat down at the table with the Professor, box and all, concealed in his lap.

'Exercise Fifty-Five – you got as far as number eleven,' said Miss Simkin. 'Begin at number twelve.'

Michael began copying it out of the book very slowly. After a minute Miss Simkin went out of the room. Instantly Michael picked up a pair of compasses and began very delicately prising at the gum.

'Open your mouth as wide as you can,' he whispered, 'it's loosening.'

The Professor stretched his mouth and stared at the ceiling.

Miss Simkin came back. 'Don't sit with your hands in your lap, Michael. Get on with the problem.'

'I was just thinking what I ought to do next.'

She came and looked over his shoulder and he leaned forward.

'Multiply each side by 5x.' She moved back.

Michael glanced down and saw the Professor valiantly sitting with his mouth wide open, to prevent the gum from sticking to his upper teeth. He burst into a shout of laughter.

'What are you laughing at, Michael?'

'I was only thinking how queer a rat would look if it swallowed a cough drop and had to sit with its mouth open.'

'Well stop thinking about such silly things and get on.'

Michael multiplied each side by 5x, did a little tinkering, and produced an answer of minus-five-and-three-sixteenths-x. He passed the book over.

'You've got this quite wrong, Michael. In the first place the answer shouldn't be in x's at all. What are you doing in your lap?'

'Playing with my compasses.'

'Well put them on the table. Do it again correctly while I go downstairs.' The door shut behind her and Michael really got to work on the Professor. At last the gummy cough drop came loose and fell out on the palm of Michael's hand.

'Ach! My poor throat!' Nicodemus sighed shrilly.

'My goodness! Here comes Miss Simkin again! I must do that sum.'

Michael popped the Professor back in his box.

'You are slow, Michael. Do hurry up!' she said impatiently. 'I believe you spend the time when I'm out of the room just gazing out of the window.' Michael felt this was unjust. He finished the sum and even managed to get it right. Mickle, curled up by the fire, went to sleep, and the rain beat softly on the window.

During the next lesson Michael's ear caught the sound of the Professor clearing his throat. 'I do hope he's all right,' Michael thought anxiously.

At last lunchtime came, Miss Simkin went off to her own room, and Michael hastily opened the box and asked the Professor how he was.

'My throat it ache terribly,' he said in a plaintive tone.

'Do you want some Diatherma?' asked Mickle.

'Plee-eese,' said Nicodemus faintly.

'What's Diatherma?' whispered Michael.

'You wouldn't have come across it,' said Mickle. 'It's about the best cure for nose and throat troubles there is.'

'But where do you get it?'

'Oh, it's a plant. It grows in Mador's Wood, so you'd better get some after lunch. The Professor needs it badly, I should say.'

As soon as lunch was over Michael walked through streaming rain to Mador's Wood, five miles away, since Minerva said she was too stiff and lame to carry him.

The Diatherma was not easy to find, but finally he recognized it from Mickle's description by its black triangular leaves with their pale edgings, picked a good bunch, and started the long walk home.

Mickle met him in the hall and hurried upstairs ahead of him. They had arranged never to speak in public places. In the schoolroom he said, 'Let's see how much you've got. Yes, that'll do. Chop the leaves into a mash and boil them up with a cupful of water. Then skim off the scum (that has quite a different use) and boil again with an equal amount of potash.'

'Where shall I get the potash?'

'How should I know?' snapped Mickle. 'That's your business. Try asking the gardener.'

Michael set a saucepan on the fire. Then he went out looking for potash. As the Diatherma cooked it gave out the most unspeakably awful smell.

'Excellent,' said Mickle, presently, looking at the green porridge. 'Be careful what you do with the scum; mind you get it all off. It has a most powerful effect.'

After the scum had been skimmed and the mixture reboiled, Michael tipped it into a little jar that had once held acid drops.

'What shall I do with the scum?'

'Oh put it on the compost heap. It can't do any harm there.'

Michael was disinclined to go out into the rain again, and hid it, for the time being, in his private cupboard in a candy box lid.

'If the medicine is cool you can give the Professor three drops on a knitting needle,' said Mickle. So three drops of what looked like green treacle were glugged down the Professor's throat, and almost at once he began to feel better.

'I weel seet a leetle by the fire,' he said, 'and you weel be so kind as to put in my box a leetle piece of flannel – no? I seet in a draught, I theenk – eet ees not good, at my age.' So Michael found a piece left over from his red dressing gown and made Nicodemus a snug sleeping bag into which he presently retired.

Mickle was dozing, and Michael himself felt more and more sleepy after the late night and all the exercise. When James came in with the supper-tray he found the Prince fast asleep beside Mickle, with his head on a cushion.

6

When Mickle asked the Professor after supper whether the Prince knew enough elementary Brock to come along that evening and have a talk with his friend the badger, Nicodemus shook his head.

'No,' he said decisively. 'Brock ees a special dialect. Veree guttural. The Preence has not yet mastered the scrape in the throat, back of the gulleet. By tomorrow, when I shall have geev heem another lesson, yes. Tonight, no.'

Mickle scolded impatiently, but as Minerva was out of action too, there was no help for it, so Michael settled down to a lesson in the curious guttural grunts, rasps, and yarlings of badger language.

Anyway it was still pouring.

When he went to bed he remembered the Diatherma scum. Should he have thrown it away? Would it be eating through the lid? He took it out of the cupboard. To his surprise it had cleared and hardened into the most beautiful dark green gum, with a scent like pine needles, firm as rubber. A longing came over him to taste it; it looked like the most delightful candy. Surely it could do him no harm? He cut it in two, and put one of the halves in his mouth. It melted, but to his disappointment had almost no taste; just the faintest aromatic breath. It seemed harmless enough, and he concluded it would be safe to leave the other piece in the cupboard overnight.

Next morning he was awakened by Mickle jumping on his chest.

'Did you eat some of that Diatherma scum?'

'Yes. Why?'

'Look at yourself in the glass, that's all.'

He got unwillingly out of bed and went to the long mirror on the wardrobe door. Then he rubbed his eyes and stared, walking from side to side. He turned to Mickle and said,

'I can't see myself.'

'Precisely,' said Mickle drily.

'Have I gone blind?'

'No, my good child. You're invisible.'

'*Invisible?* What fun,' said Michael. 'I'll get Miss Simkin to give me a holiday – I daresay she won't mind for once, as it would be such hard work teaching someone you couldn't see – and we'll go and see Brock.'

'I shouldn't wait to speak to Miss Simkin,' said Mickle.

'Write her a note. It will be wiser not to let anyone know what's happened.'

'How long will it last?' Michael asked.

'How much did you eat?'

'Not a very big piece, about this size.'

'Oh, that's all right then,' said Mickle, relieved. 'It shouldn't take more than a day to wear off. But do be more careful about the things you eat. It's so *human* to do a thing like that. Now you'd better steal some breakfast out of the larder – you can't eat it in the breakfast room with your royal parents. They'd have a fit if they saw bacon mysteriously disappearing from dishes, and think the invasion had begun.'

They went down the back stairs to the kitchen where, as it was still early, the kitchen staff were sitting comfortably eating breakfast and talking. It was gloriously warm. Michael stood in front of the great stove, to listen and enjoy his invisibility. He had to be very quick in dodging out of people's way when they walked towards him, and once had his foot stepped on by the butler, who glanced down in a puzzled manner.

Mickle gave a nudge to the Prince's leg. 'Go on – forage,' he said in the Universal Animal Language.

Michael went into the larder, where he ate some bread and butter and cherry jam tarts. Then he took a cold chicken and some fresh rolls and butter for his day's supplies.

He returned to the kitchen and found Mickle licking his chops after the last of two trout the cook had given him.

Outside in the garden the Prince wrote a note for Miss Simkin:

'Dear Miss Simkin, I am afraid I shall not be in today as I am called out on urgent public business, so please take a holiday. Yours sincerely, Michael P.'

They went round by the front door and he put the note on the hall table. It became visible as he let go of it.

'Now, what shall we do first?'

'We'll go and talk to Minerva.'

But as they went through the gardens they found Minerva, looking extremely indignant, harnessed to a large rake which she was drawing across the lawn.

'Nice work for my old age!' she exclaimed crossly. 'You ought to speak to your father about it, Michael.'

'I will when I'm visible,' said Michael. 'But how did you know I was here?'

'My good boy, I can hear you and smell you, can't I?' Minerva said. 'Well, where are you off to?'

'Going to see Brock. Can you come?'

'I can't neglect my duty, can I?' grumbled Minerva perversely. 'You'll have to manage without me.' And to all their persuasions she turned a deaf ear.

'How shall we get there?' asked Michael. 'Didn't you say it was a long way?'

'My collar gives me wishes,' Mickle explained. And he wished for a conveyance to take them to Dingle Warren.

Instantly, two enchanting little scarlet chariots whirled down out of the sky. Each was drawn by a fire-breathing dragon. Michael thought them so lovely that all he could do was stand and gaze, but Mickle jumped into his chariot, snapped, 'Dingle Warren, double quick,' and was whisked off, so the Prince hastily climbed into his and said, 'Follow that chariot.'

A couple of starlings were much upset at the sight of Mickle's equipage, and skittered away downwind chattering indignant remarks at each other. 'It didn't ought to be allowed,' they said. 'Cats in the air! What next?'

Fairly soon they came to the Dingle Warren country, which was low and flat, a network of woods and swampy fields. Suddenly as the chariots turned in a long curve towards the ground, an awful thought struck Michael.

'I say,' he shouted, 'do you know we came away in such a hurry I forgot to give the Professor any breakfast?'

'Oh lord, that won't do,' said Mickle. 'We must send a message back and ask someone to feed him. After all, he's doing us a kindness in staying.'

'Miss Simkin would feed him, I expect,' Michael said, 'if she knew. She disapproves of keeping wild animals as pets, and she's very keen on seeing they're properly treated.'

'Write her another note,' Mickle said, 'and ask a rook to fly over with it.'

Their chariots landed, and vanished at once. Michael wrote his note, and looked round for rooks. A flock of them was tumbling about over some trees not far away.

'Just call "Come here,"' Mickle said. 'Your U.A.L. is good enough for that, I hope.'

Michael went rather pink and felt a fool, but summoned up resolution when he thought of the poor Professor, hungry and breakfastless.

'Come here,' he called to the rooks, and added, 'if you don't mind.'

Much to his surprise they all came, playing a game of tag on the way over, and landing around him with a series of bouncing thumps, to look at him with bright beady eyes.

'Chawmed to make your acquaintance, I'm shewer,' said one who seemed to be the leader. He was smaller than the others, and looked very knowing and witty. 'Don't often speak to invisible humans, do we boys?'

'I wondered if you'd mind doing something for me,' said Michael politely. 'I urgently need a letter carried to my governess at the Palace.'

'There, I said so, didn't I, cullies?' exclaimed the leader rook triumphantly. 'I said it was the Prince when we saw you flying past with that perditioned great cat of yours – ahem, begging your pardon and no harm intended.' He winked teasingly in the direction of Mickle, who was studiously taking no notice.

Michael handed over the note.

'We'll find her okay,' said the leader, taking it in his beak, and the others echoed, 'Okay, okay, okay,' rising about Michael until the air was full of cawing and flapping.

'It's very kind of you,' Michael called.

'No trouble – good for the liver, a little flight first thing. Any time you want something done, Lord Porty's the name.'

'What a jolly lot,' Michael said, when they had flown off.

'Ye-es,' said Mickle, giving his ear a polish. 'A little too merry and bright for my taste.' He strolled off through the swampy and tangled wood towards a sandbank which ran out beside a little river.

'Brock lives somewhere about here,' he said, and sniffed at a large hole in the bank.

At that moment an elegant black and white head appeared out of some bushes and looked at them keenly.

7

'Well, well,' said Brock, coming out of the bush, 'if it isn't Mickle. What brings you out at such a peculiar time, Mickle, and who have you got with you?' He sniffed suspiciously at Michael's invisible legs.

'This is Prince Michael,' the cat explained. 'He's invisible at the moment, but he's quite harmless.'

'Does he speak Brock?'

'Passably, I believe.'

'How do you do, Prince. I don't think much of your calling hours, but I'm delighted to meet you.'

'Were you just going to bed?' Michael said. 'I'm so sorry.'

'We've come to ask you to help us,' Mickle cut in.

'Well,' Brock said, 'what can I do for you gentlemen?'

'We want to know if you can tell us anything about some people who live underground.'

'How did you know that story?' Brock said in surprise. 'I thought no one knew it but us burrowers, and we keep pretty quiet about it.'

'So there is a story?' said Michael in excitement.

'There certainly is. You've come to the right person to hear about it, too.'

'You've met them, then?'

'I have,' said Brock, 'and I don't much care to think about it even now. Ugh.' He moved his head uneasily. 'However I'll tell you about it.' He gave a rasp, deep in his throat, hunched himself comfortably against the sandbank, and began.

'It was about two winters ago. I was living in a sandpit not far from here. One night there was a shocking storm – sleet, rain, and gale – and as I was coming home a large piece of the cliff broke away under me. I tumbled down the cliff in a sort of landslide and somehow – don't ask me how, for it was as dark as pitch and even I couldn't see a thing – I must have fallen down a kind of pot-hole. I found myself being swept along, at hurtling speed, in an underground river. Couldn't possibly swim, but at last I was washed ashore in a big cave. It was almost pitch dark but I managed to see some things – big things – *houses*. They were enormous. They went right up to the roof of the cave, and that was higher than the highest pine tree. All solid black rock. There was something dreadful about them – little cracks for windows and dreadful people inside.

'I thought, even though there was a smell of magic about, that I should be safe enough in the dark, but suddenly, taking me by surprise, the whole place became light. Awful! A harsh white glare from the ceiling of the cave. Of course I was dazed and dazzled and was easily caught.'

'By whom?' asked Michael in great excitement.

'By some people in black – Under People. Horrible people. They kept me in a box, and used to let me out sometimes and set their dogs on me.'

He stopped and growled to himself, and Mickle's tail swelled in sympathy.

'I finished off some of their dogs, though.

'At last I managed to escape. The white light used to go on and off regularly – sort of artificial days and nights – and one time I'd just knocked over a wretched little cur when everything went dark, so I dashed away. They all came yoohooing after me, but I made for the smell of water and found the underground river. I jumped in, was carried away by the current, and must have knocked my head on a rock, for I lost consciousness. Later I found myself in broad daylight lying on a sandbank in the Grune River near Little Pol.'

'Did you ever go back to the sandpit to look for the hole you'd fallen into?'

'I did, yes, but there had been a big landslide and the hole was blocked – there was just a heap of earth and rock.'

Michael's face fell.

'Do you think—' he began, but both Mickle and Brock were sitting bolt upright, sniffing the air alertly.

'Excuse me,' muttered Brock, and in half a second he had disappeared into the very middle of a clump of gorse. A minute later a gamekeeper and his dog came into the pit. The Prince picked up Mickle, who was hissing terribly, and tucked him under his arm, out of harm's way.

The keeper saw the cat suddenly rise about four feet into the air and stay suspended. He gave a yell of terror and rushed away from the path, the dog scuttling after him. When they were gone, Michael said,

'Where's Brock, do you suppose?'

'I shouldn't think we shall see him again today,' said Mickle. 'He can't abide dogs.'

He was quite right. Though they hunted high and low through the wood there was no sign of him.

They ate their provisions and explored the sandpit at the other end of the wood, but it was as Brock had said; any opening there might have been was completely choked by a huge landslide.

'What shall we do? Hunt along the banks of the Grune River for the place where he came out?'

'No, that's too vague,' Mickle said. 'It might take weeks. I think before we start exploring underground we want to know a bit more history.'

'History?'

'Yes; I have a plan about that, but I can't do anything till tomorrow. It will be All Cats' Night; we can go to Bare Hill and ask a Question.'

This was quite unintelligible to Michael, and he was about to ask a question then and there, when Mickle went on,

'In the meantime we may as well hunt for the cave under the waterfall where they hid the treasure. We want that located – it may be an entrance to the Underground Country too. How's your bird dialect getting on?'

'It's not bad,' said Michael. 'All except Nightingale. Why?'

'Could you understand detailed directions?'

'I think so.'

'There's an old pheasant called Spargoin in the Palace grounds,' Mickle said. 'He and I don't exactly hit it off, but he's a wise old bird and knows a lot about the geography of Astalon. It might be worth asking him about the waterfall – so long as you don't mention my name.'

They had been picking their way through the wood, and at this moment Mickle got his tail entangled in some dead burrs and the Prince had to come to his help.

'I wish to goodness we were out of this miserable wood!' exclaimed Mickle furiously. Immediately an unseen force picked them up and dropped them in the Palace gardens.

Michael was becoming visible in patches.

'You can't go indoors looking like that,' Mickle said, surveying him critically. '*Anyone* would smell a rat.'

'But I want my tea.'

'Your family would think you'd been bewitched. You can't have your tea just yet. I'll go in and tell the Professor you're back, and you wait in the shrubbery till you're fit to be seen. Shouldn't be more than an hour – maybe less. You might see if you can find Spargoin while you're waiting.'

Michael sat down rather disconsolately in the shrubbery on a mossy patch which was not so soft as it looked. He gave a low, throaty pheasant call and waited. After a few minutes, rather to his surprise a peevish-looking old pheasant came stepping cautiously through the brambles.

'Hullo,' said Michael softly, 'are you Spargoin?'

'Yes, I am Spargoin, though I don't know why I should have to tell the fact to every dratted boy that comes jabbering pidgin-pheasant to me in broad daylight. Well, what do *you* want?'

Michael apologized very humbly and explained that he wanted to know the whereabouts of a certain place, and he had heard that Spargoin would be bound to know.

'Well, what is this place?'

'It's a waterfall,' the Prince explained, 'between two lakes, with some yew-trees round it, and it has a cave under it with a stream coming out of the cave.'

Spargoin said, rather unwillingly, 'Yes, I know where it is. Look, scrape some of the moss away and I'll draw a map. Heavens, no, child, larger than that.'

Michael obediently scraped a large clear patch, and Spargoin began moving about on it, clucking to himself. 'H'm, let's see. This is Witches' Wood. Give me a stone – yes, that'll do. Put it there – no, more to the right. Can't you see where I am pointing? Now a piece of grass here, and a dead leaf there.'

Michael arranged sticks and straws, and Spargoin scraped with his claw in the soft earth. Finally quite an intricate looking map was produced.

'There,' said Spargoin, 'now attend, because if there's one thing I hate, it's having to repeat myself. I suppose you can fly? No? You humans are shockingly incompetent.'

'I might be able to,' said Michael, thinking of the dragon chariots, 'but I don't think I could guarantee it.'

'Tt,tt,tt,' said Spargoin, 'fancy not even knowing whether you could or not.' He looked extremely disapproving.

'I think it would be safer if you told me the way along the ground.'

It was a long and complicated route, and as the landmarks were mostly more suitable for pheasants than humans, Michael hoped devoutly he would be able to remember them all. Spargoin concluded:

'You turn into the wood by three white stones, come out where there's a rotten log with a rabbit burrow at one end ... That brings you out just below the waterfall, and then the cave entrance is here. There's supposed to be another entrance to it in the swamp beside the lower lake, but I don't know it. There, I've told you everything, probably a lot more than you deserve.'

The old pheasant turned and vanished into a bed of nettles.

Michael sat down and, pulling out his notebook, made as good a copy of the map as he could. Then he had another look at his arms and legs and decided that though he still appeared rather pale he could go into the Palace without exciting alarm or suspicion. Anyway, dusk was falling.

On his way upstairs he met Miss Simkin.

'*There* you are,' she said irritably. 'I suppose you decided to stay away all day because I told you yesterday you'd be having an algebra test.'

Michael looked at her guiltily. He had forgotten all about it.

8

Miss Simkin was extremely angry, and told Michael he would have to do the test next day, although it was Saturday. She lectured him all the way up to the school-room, and left him, saying that he could certainly not have banana fritters for supper. Michael was quite astonished.

'I'd have thought she'd enjoy a holiday,' he said to Mickle. 'It's a frightful nuisance because now I won't be able to come and look for the waterfall tomorrow morning.'

'Then we'd better go tonight,' Mickle said. 'We can't afford to waste any time, I'm sure. Did you get the directions from Spargoin all right? Did you discover how far it is?'

'Not exactly, because he measures distances by flying-time, but it seems to be a long way. We'd better eat a large supper, even if it isn't banana fritters,' Michael said.

'Minerva says she's too tired to go anywhere tonight, after all that lawn-raking. Apparently they kept her at it all day;

it's really too bad. We'll use my collar, but we'd better get some sleep first.'

They both went to bed immediately after the fritterless supper. Mickle was asleep at once, and the Prince soon followed his example. He woke with a start at midnight, when Mickle prodded his chest, gave a huge yawn, and followed sleepily to the window.

'Wake up properly, for goodness' sake,' said Mickle sharply, 'I don't want you falling and breaking your neck.' So Michael shook himself awake, and, leaning out, gulped in several breaths of damp, fresh air.

'Now,' said Mickle, 'I want something to carry us to the waterfall – we'll tell you the way as we go. Do you understand?'

'That's clever,' said Michael admiringly. 'But why do we have to tell the way?'

Mickle was already jumping into his carriage – a little silver Surrey with a fringe on top – while Michael's hovered in mid air waiting for him. As soon as he was in, it soared up to Mickle's.

'Now, fire away with your notebook,' said Mickle.

'Why do we have to tell them the way?' said Michael again, after he had given the first directions.

'Because, when you're using magic, you always have to know exactly what you want or it's no good,' Mickle replied. 'If we had been to the waterfall before, we could say "Take us there" and that would be enough, because the knowledge of the way would be inside our minds and conveyed in our wish. But if you haven't been to a place, then there's nothing in your mind, and the only thing you can do is to give the directions from the map.'

'Turn left here,' said Michael, peering anxiously at the country below.

'That's why,' Mickle went on, as if he were giving a lecture, 'we can't just say "Take us to the treasure," and have done with it, because we don't know where it is.'

Michael sighed; he felt that the rules of magic were very tiresome, almost as unaccountable as those of algebra.

It was rather dreamlike to be dashing at such a speed through the night sky, flicking in and out of banks of cloud. After about twenty minutes' rapid flying they dropped towards the ground, whipping in between trees at an alarming rate. Both carriages then landed as lightly as birds settling, and Michael hopped out into the darkness. To his disgust he sank up to his ankles in mud.

'Don't get down,' he said to Mickle, who was peering out, 'it's boggy. Where are we, anyway?'

'I reckon these are the swamps by the lower lake. There it is, over there – we can just follow it up to the waterfall. You carry me, and walk slowly, so that I can tell you where to put your feet. Don't go away,' he commanded the carriages, 'wait here till we're ready to go back.'

After some hazardous and squelchy walking they began to hear the roar of the waterfall and found firm ground where a path ran down into the swamp to meet them.

'There are the yew-trees,' exclaimed Mickle. 'The cave entrance must be near here.' He jumped from Michael's arms on to the harder ground, which was carpeted with needles. 'I remember the picture of that big yew with three branches. There's the stream that comes out of the cave.'

He was really excited, although he pretended to be calm; his tail was upright and quivering as he galloped along the bank of the stream.

They rounded the largest yew-tree and stopped short in disappointment. Where the cave entrance should have been there was only a large muddy and rocky smear down the face of the bank, through which the stream made a trickling course.

'There must have been a fall of rock here, too, since the people went into the cave,' said Mickle coldly and calmly, 'and the entrance is blocked.' They stood and stared at it for a couple of minutes.

'There must be some way in,' said Michael at last. He climbed over a pile of clay and stones and hunted along the face of the bank. But there was not a sign of a hole.

'Well,' he said sadly, coming back, 'it's no use staying here now. We can come tomorrow afternoon with a spade, perhaps, and dig. Maybe we can find Spargoin's other entrance – there's one in the swamp somewhere. It's too dark now, and it's starting to rain.'

The rain beat softly in their faces as the carriages raced back, and once Michael thought he felt an owl brush past him. When they reached the Palace the carriages hovered outside his window and Mickle jumped neatly across the gap. The Prince climbed in more cautiously.

'Shut those west windows,' said Mickle, digging himself a nest in the eiderdown, 'or you'll hear from Miss Simkin if the rain comes in.'

'There's already a pool of water on the windowsill,' said Michael giggling. He hurried out of his clothes and jumped into bed. A minute later he was asleep.

It had rained itself out by next morning and was brilliantly fine. Michael sat irritably doing his algebra test and looking out at the sunlit garden. He felt like rushing through it and going out, but Mickle had said sharply to him that he was to do it decently; there was no sense in being kept in all afternoon to do it again. So he was being as careful as he could, helped by the companionship of Nicodemus, who was sunning himself on the windowsill and attending to his toilet.

'You shouldn't have pets out while you're doing lessons,' said Miss Simkin.

'Oh, but he doesn't help me at all,' Michael protested. 'He doesn't know any algebra. Languages are his strong point.'

'Well I hope you remembered to feed him today,' she said sourly.

She was pleasantly surprised, however, at his good results, and remarked, 'I wish you always did your algebra like this.'

'Perhaps my holiday did me good,' he suggested.

'As a matter of fact I was thinking you looked pale. Are you all right?'

'Yes, yes,' said Michael, dying to be off. She was looking at him rather suspiciously, and he kept his finger-tips, which were still invisible, concealed under the table.

'Very well, you may go,' she said at last.

Mickle was not in the garden, so he went to Minerva's field, and found the two of them deep in talk.

'Well, I don't like it at all,' Minerva was saying. 'If you ask me, it's downright foolhardy.'

'What is?' asked Michael, leaning against the gate.

'We've been arguing,' said Minerva placidly. They were all three rather drowsy and good tempered in the warm autumn sunshine.

'I want to go and have another look at the waterfall,' explained Mickle, 'and see if we can find that other entrance.'

'And *I* say,' Minerva broke in, 'that it's stupid to go looking inside caves before you know what you're up against. From what Mickle tells me Brock said, I reckon those people underground are a very nasty lot, and I'd want to know a bit more about how they got there, and the best way to deal with them, before I went trotting down among them.'

'Yes,' said Mickle, 'but we don't *know* that the waterfall cave leads to their country, and we do know that it's where the treasure was hidden.'

'But even if we find the treasure,' argued Minerva, 'I can't see that it will help against the Downstairs people. We may find that this invention of Michael's great-grandfather is quite useless to us.'

'I know,' said Mickle patiently, as if he had said the same thing several times before, 'but we've been to all the people who can give us information, and there *was* the saying that it would help the kingdom in its darkest hour. The only remaining source of information is by the Question, at the cats' meeting tonight on Bare Hill. Meanwhile we might as well be doing something.'

Michael entirely agreed.

'Suppose we just go over and *look* for the entrance,' he said. 'After all, it might need digging or widening, you know, and even if we find the way in, we needn't go in at once. We could mark it on the map, so that we can get there by magic collar when we want to. Then we can come back and ask your Question.'

'That's sense,' said Mickle, and even Minerva had to agree that it seemed fairly harmless.

'As long as you don't go forgetting and dashing in.'

'Before we go, I think you had better put the Professor back in his stream,' said Mickle. 'He has taught you enough for our purposes, and as we may be engaged in a lot of hazardous operations soon, I'd be easier in my mind if he wasn't shut up in a box and likely to die of starvation.'

Michael saw the force of this, though he felt he would miss the Professor's friendly presence in the schoolroom.

Nicodemus was delighted at the thought of once more exchanging the great draughty Palace for his snug little stream.

'It was very kind of you to come and teach me,' Michael said.

'A treefle, a treefle,' the Professor replied, waving his tail modestly. 'I have learned some interesting human dialect.'

There was a tiny stream in the orchard, with peppermint and forgetmenots on the banks.

'Up at the top eend,' Nicodemus directed Michael. He was quivering with pleasure at the familiar smells, and kept nearly jumping out of Michael's hands. 'By a beeg stone, I leev.'

Michael knelt and put the Professor carefully on the big stone. He stretched himself, looking about with the alert pleasure of one who has been away for many years. 'Ah! Eet has changed!'

Michael could not see that the stream and grass bank

were in the slightest degree different, but the Professor's sharp eyes caught sight of many alterations: a large stick which had stuck against a stone and hung, making a long v-shaped ripple across the current, a clod of earth fallen from the bank; a little pile of dead walnut leaves drifted down against a sand bar. Nicodemus looked and looked, and then dived neatly into the water with no splash, just a faint plop. He reappeared with every whisker glistening.

'Ah! The water!' he said joyfully to Michael. 'That was what I needed!'

'Isn't it bad for your throat?' said Michael doubtfully, dipping his hand in the ice-cold current.

'Never!' said Nicodemus. 'Air, that ees bad. Always blowing hot, cold, wheestle, wheestle, from all doors and weendows. But water ees always the same; when eet change, eet change gradual.' And he vanished for another glorious dive. Michael rather shyly put a present of some dried cherries on a stone.

'Oh, how kieend,' cried the Professor radiantly. 'Now I must go and seek my friends; they will theenk an owl has eaten me. Come and veesit me whenever you are down this way.' He waved his tail and dived, and this time he did not reappear.

Michael walked away feeling a little sad. 'Bother,' he thought, 'I never asked how he did Mickle a good turn. I must remember to find out next time I see him.' The idea cheered him. After all, not many people had a friend who lived in a stream at the bottom of the orchard.

He told the King and Queen that he was going off for the afternoon, and it seemed to him that they welcomed the news. In fact they were so worried these days that trying to keep up an appearance of cheerfulness in front of Michael was a great strain.

'*He* looks all right, anyway,' said the Queen, sighing.

'Deep in some mysterious plot, no doubt,' agreed the King indulgently – and then suddenly had a horrible qualm as he thought of the prophecy: 'Your son will go alone among them.'

Michael took a small spade with him, and a pick, in case digging was necessary; besides these items Minerva was disgusted to see that he had remembered her saddle and bridle.

'Horrible heavy things,' she muttered discontentedly as he girthed her up.

'I'm sorry,' said Michael, 'but it does make a difference, you know, when I have to carry Mickle and all the other things.' He fastened the tools on his bag of provisions, slung it on his back, picked up Mickle, and mounted without too much difficulty, though Minerva complained that the spade had slapped her.

But none of them could really feel downcast on such a fine day, and they jogged off in the sunshine more as if it was an ordinary picnic than a nationally important journey of exploration.

Minerva sang a tuneless little song, in time to which she clattered along:

> They makes you trot along the roads,
>   They hits you if you stops,
> They sings and shouts and blows their horns,
>   They don't care if you drops.

> They jumps you over thorny gaps,
>   They gallops you through gorse,
> You never gets a word of thanks,
>   Who'd be a poor old horse?

Michael felt rather guilty when he heard this, and had to give Minerva lumps of sugar to allay his conscience, but Mickle was scornful.

'I've never yet met a horse who didn't complain he had a dog's life,' he said, 'but it's just to show off. Why, if they didn't like to be ridden they could perfectly well do something about it; they're a lot stronger than humans. But they'd much rather be ridden than have to scratch about and find their own living.'

Minerva sniffed, but said nothing.

The journey to the waterfall took much longer on foot than by magic carriage, and they were all hungry and hot when they arrived. Minerva was cross because she had been made to swim the river, so they decided to have lunch at once. Michael and the cat sat on a dry rock above the waterfall, and Minerva wandered about nearby. The Prince had thoughtfully brought along some oats, so she soon became pleasant again.

Michael dangled his legs in the water which rushed smoothly and silently through a narrow rocky channel above the fall. Just as he took his last bite he gave a sharp exclamation.

'What's the matter?' said Mickle.

'There's something alive tangled about my legs. It feels like a snake.'

He wriggled his feet and pulled them out of the water. Snarled about them was a large eel, which looked at him in surprise and said,

'I beg your pardon. I seem to be tied in a knot. It's this shocking current which quite swept me away. If you'll be so kind as to wait a moment or two, I think I can get myself untied.'

Michael was so taken back to hear an eel speak, and to be able to understand it, that he sat perfectly still with his mouth open while the eel slowly and carefully untangled herself. Then his good manners returned, and he apologized politely in the basic fish language.

'Not at all,' said the eel, 'my fault entirely. Are you having a picnic? Charming weather, isn't it?'

'We were looking—' said Michael, and then an idea came to him. 'I suppose you don't happen to know the where-abouts of the second entrance to the cave under the waterfall? The one near here is blocked up.'

'Blocked, is it,' she said thoughtfully. 'I've not been that way for some time. I keep up above the fall as a rule.'

She was a very polite creature. She locked her tail firmly round a rock, swung out into the current, and pondered about caves for some time in silence. At length she said, 'I remember my mamma once told me of her great-great-grandmother hearing of some men being trapped in the cave by a landslide. (They're rather common round here, you know.) Great-great-great-grandmamma was rather annoyed, because the cave had been a pet haunt of hers for thinking in – nice and dark, you know, and cool. She was fond of going about on land and visiting odd places. She took to looking for another entrance, and finally found one.'

'Where?' asked Michael eagerly.

The eel looked a little doubtful. She reared herself out of the water and pointed with her head, using her tail as a rudder to keep herself steady. 'It was over in that direction in the marshes. I'd come with you, but I'm slow on land, and it isn't really my country down there.'

'Oh, no, please don't trouble,' said Michael politely. He was not sure how she would get on with Mickle, who so far had kept himself tactfully behind a rock. 'It's very kind of you to have been so helpful. Can I carry you back to the upper lake?'

'Well,' said the eel, 'if you wouldn't mind, it would be a kindness. I'm not as young as I was, and I can't deny that this current is powerful.'

So Michael carefully picked her up – she was surprisingly heavy and frightfully slippery – and carried her, dangling and slithering, up the path, over the road that bridged the fall, and to the verge of the lake on the other side, where he dropped her in. She thanked him, wished him good luck, and disappeared silently into the dark muddy depths.

Then suddenly her head came out again.

'Butcher's Broom,' she shouted.

'I beg your pardon?'

'Butcher's Broom. There's a lot of it growing round the cave entrance. My great-great-great-grandma was terribly inconvenienced by the prickles.'

'Oh, thank you very much. I'll look out for that,' said Michael, and she vanished again.

He went back to his companions.

'A fat lot of chance we have of finding the cave,' grumbled Minerva, 'on the word of an eel's great-grandmother. If you ask me, we'll be hunting about these marshes for weeks.'

It was a dreary place. The marshes were all overgrown with rushes, and tall reedy grass, high banks of nettles, clumps of willows and alders. They had to cover every foot of the ground in order to make sure they had not missed the entrance. Backwards and forwards they wandered.

'I must say,' said Michael gloomily after several hours, 'when you stop to think, it's not often you find a cave in a swamp. The water would just run in and fill it.'

'Well, we've practically covered the whole area now,' said Mickle, some time later. 'We'll come to higher ground soon.'

They moved on with difficulty, looking wearily about.

'There's a bank over there,' said Michael. 'See? All grown

over with holly bushes. There might be Butcher's Broom too – they grow in the same sort of places.'

The ground was rising into a sandy wood of oak and hazel, low-lying, with clumps of reeds, but solid to the foot and not so overgrown as the swamp. They quickened their pace towards the bank.

'It's almost a cliff,' said Michael, panting. He was on foot, giving Minerva a rest by carrying Mickle and the tools.

The bank was nearly perpendicular, smooth red sandstone. A little rivulet ran down it, dripping long streamers of moss, and disappeared into the swamp.

'Look! Butcher's Broom!' Michael shouted, and pointed to some thick dark clumps ahead, with large red berries among the spiky leaves. Mickle suddenly jumped out of the Prince's hold and raced ahead.

'Has he seen something?' asked Minerva, craning her neck. She and the Prince hurried round an outcrop in the bank and found Mickle sitting triumphantly in front of a deep, narrow opening in the red stone.

9

'Does it go in far?' asked Michael breathlessly, leaning on the spade.

'You can't see,' Mickle answered. Michael went to the opening and peered in, but before he could take another step Minerva had grabbed the back of his shirt with her teeth and yanked him away from temptation.

'Put it on the map and let's go home,' she said. 'Or I know how it'll be. The two of you will be hanging round that door and saying 'One step inside wouldn't do any harm,' and then it'll be three steps and five steps, and before you know where you are, you *won't* know where you are.'

So Michael pulled out his notebook and marked the lower swamp and the ridge and cave entrance on his map.

'There must be a shorter way back to the road than that terrific circle we took through the swamp,' he said. 'If we keep along the top of the ridge we ought to strike it farther back.'

'Or we might get lost,' Mickle grumbled, but Minerva said she was sick of going along up to her hocks in mud. Anyone who liked could go back through the swamp, *she* was going along the ridge. Sure enough, after passing through some more sandy oak-woods they were able to drop down on the road about half a mile before it reached the waterfall.

'Well at least we know the shortest way home from here,' Michael said, 'thank goodness. I've never been so scratched and hungry and muddy and thirsty and bitten and stung in all my life before.'

'All just to find a wretched cave, probably with nothing inside it,' Minerva said, but more to herself than aloud, and she started off at a fair pace, only turning her head once to observe, 'I think I deserve a bran mash for this, Michael.'

'You shall have one,' said Michael fervently, 'or two if you like.'

That evening at dinner Michael said to the King, 'Was my grandfather an inventor like you, Father?'

'He did a bit of inventing,' the King said gloomily. He looked deathly tired. 'It's always been in the family.'

'What did he invent?'

'Oh – among other things, an everlasting torch: a tube full of luminous fluid. It's only the size of your finger but it lights a whole room.'

'Doesn't it ever fade?'

'It's good for about forty-eight hours. And unless you're at the North Pole it's never dark for as long as that.'

'It sounds as if it would be a useful thing to have,' said Michael. 'What did great-grandpa invent?'

'Oh, lots of small things. His best invention was lost,' said the King slowly. 'No one ever knew what it was, but it was thought to have been some kind of weapon, because he said it would save the kingdom in its darkest hour.'

'Oh, how—'

'Michael!' the Queen interrupted. 'It's high time you went upstairs. Finish that apple and you can take some grapes with you.'

Michael was allowed to stay up to late dinner on Saturdays, but he ate his dessert in his own room. He put a quarter of apple into his mouth.

'How did it get lost?' he said hurriedly. But the King frowned and said,

'Yes, Michael, it's high time you were in bed.'

He kissed his parents goodnight and ran upstairs, calling in at Mickle's room.

'Come along,' he hissed, and raced on.

'What's all the excitement?' asked Mickle, when they were safely in Michael's room. The Prince told him what his father had said.

'Interesting, isn't it?'

'It certainly seems to confirm what we had gathered already. If only we knew what this precious invention was.'

'I don't think Father knew – though Mother was making faces at him in case he said anything I'm too young to hear.'

Mickle sniffed. 'I don't know who'd be trying to do anything about all this trouble if you weren't,' he said. 'It's a good thing you aren't such a young nitwit as your parents seem to imagine.

'Anyway we'll try and find out the whole business tonight. I've been out to Minerva but she says thank you kindly, she's had as much exercise as she can do with for one day and we can go out magicking by ourselves. So we'll get some sleep before we start and then go the magic-collar way.'

'I do wish you'd tell me more about this Question. Where is Bare Hill?'

'You'll see when we get there.' Mickle curled up firmly, pushed his nose under his paw, and fell asleep at once. Michael followed his example.

He was awake almost as soon as Mickle prodded him with a prickly paw, and silently followed across the room to the window. When he looked out he saw that Mickle must have wished already, for a black, bat-winged leopard was hovering outside. Although it had a savage expression it purred at him, so he climbed gingerly on to its back.

'Mickle, where are you?' he whispered.

'Here,' hissed a voice above his head. Looking up he was surprised to see Mickle in mid air, hovering like the leopard.

'I never knew you could fly!' Michael exclaimed, greatly astonished. 'Why have you never done it before?'

'Hush! All cats can fly on All Cats' Night. Hurry, now.' Mickle turned and skimmed away, treading the black air lightly with his black paws.

As they flew along, something dark flashed past Michael's face and he looked quickly sideways; it seemed to him that they were not alone in the air. Other shapes were coming along with them. At first sight they were like a huge cluster of leaves blowing downwards towards a wooded hill. Another shape flitted close to his face and he saw that it was a cat. They were all cats.

By the time they landed there was a huge concourse of cats about them.

'Keep quite still,' Mickle whispered, 'don't say a word.' Michael obediently stood silent on the outskirts of the multitude of cats, looking up towards the top of the hill. More and more cats came dropping out of the sky; overhead it was black with them. He longed to ask what was going to happen but did not dare.

He did not have to wait long. Gradually he began to hear a strange humming, which grew and grew till it was like a tempestuous wind, and then faded again. It rose and died, rose and died. 'Hush!' whispered a myriad voices, 'Old Peter is coming! Make way for Old Peter, King of the Cats. Silence for the Catechism!' Then a silence, thick as felt, settled over the crowd. Michael held his breath, expecting something startling, but, as before, what came was so gradual and so quiet that he felt he had always known what it would be. It took the form of a great light, growing and glowing in the middle of the hill until he was amazed that he could keep his eyes on it.

While he was looking and dreaming, he became aware that voices were speaking. Questions were being softly asked by different speakers, and answered by one speaker – a speaker with an old, dry, furry voice, like the voice of all wisdom in cat form. Michael strained his ears, but could hear little, until the voices whispered all together, 'Silence for the Heir to the throne. Silence for His Feline Highness.' Then a voice – was it Mickle's? – put a question. Michael did not hear the first words of the answer. He was wondering about Mickle – could he really be a Prince of the cats? Then he began to listen, for what the old voice was saying now concerned him.

'Among the treasure stolen by Lord Roger was an invention of the King's. This was a ray emitted by a block of diamond which had been steeped for many years in a magical fluid. The King had not found out its full powers, but he knew that they were great, and so, to prevent unwise meddling, he kept it fastened in a box, locked with the Names of Power in a device of his own. Lord Roger was unable to open the box. It was left with the rest of the treasure after his death.

'The King never found the treasure, and he lived the rest of his life in fear that some enemy had the box. Giles Wyburn, son of Lord Roger, had escaped to foreign lands. Years later he returned, with his wicked wife, Elgitha, and a great band of companions, both men and women, meaning to recover the treasure from the cave and conquer the present King and rule over Astalon. The party journeyed by night, reached the waterfall one moonless evening, and all entered the cave together. None would remain outside in case he should be cheated of his share. They found the treasure lying where it had been left; no one had been near it since.

'When they saw that it was there, the bright reality of gold and rubies and precious things, they raised their voices in a great shout of triumph. The walls of the cave were not secure; the water had eaten away under them and they had slipped and fallen together. When this harsh noise echoed among the tunnels it loosened the balance of the rocks so that they slid down and the entrance was blocked. Search how they might, Giles and his companions could find no way out.

'At last, after digging for many hours, they broke through, not, as they had expected, to daylight, but into another vast cave, through which ran an underground river. There were fish in the river, so they were in no danger of starvation, but they could still find no way out, for the river curved away under the rock in both directions into blackness.'

The voice ceased, and Michael heard a question asked in an undertone – he thought by Mickle.

'They settled down and lived there,' the voice continued. 'They were wicked people, but brave; not the sort to perish of despair. They built houses of rock and learned to eat the underground plants and to make clothes from root fibres. They stored the King's treasure in a rock strongroom against the time when they should escape. Night and day they dug and gnawed their way along the course of the river.

'All this happened nearly eighty years ago, and by now they and their descendants have grown so accustomed to the underground life that they wish to come out only for revenge and plunder. Giles Wyburn has died. They have built a great city, and made light from subterranean sources of power, and learned an underground magic.

'They wish to conquer the Upper World and lay waste, and levy tribute. There is only one man opposed to this plan, a sage called Borlock. He asked them to wait until he had solved the secret of the magic box, but they laughed at him. 'We no longer need it,' they said. 'We have our own weapons. We shall overrun Astalon in our thousands. Throw away the box and forget it.' But Borlock begged for more time, pointing out that if they used their most powerful weapons they might blow in the roof of Down Under. Finally they gave him a hundred days in which to discover the secret. If he had not found it by the end of that time, they would begin the invasion without him. The hundred days are fast running through.'

Michael heard a voice – this time unmistakably Mickle's – ask, 'How can the box be opened? What is the secret of the ray inside it?'

'That can only be discovered by one person.'

'Who?' Mickle began, but a single clear sound, the note of a bell, sang in the air, and a different voice cried,

'The time of asking is over. The hour is near.'

The great light faded and dimmed, and many smaller lights like candle flames leaped and wavered over the crowd. The multitude of cats moved together, took shape, shifted towards the top of the hill, drew itself together—

'It's coming alive,' said Michael aloud to nothing. 'It isn't a crowd of cats, it's a—'

Crouched on the hill above him and staring down at him with flame-like slits of eyes was one enormous cat, black as night, each paw larger than a house. It rose, stretched, and lowered its head towards him.

Afterwards Michael could never remember what happened then. The sky overhead was blotted out by a great fringe of dark and he felt as if he were falling into a lake of ink. He knew nothing more.

10

When Michael returned to consciousness he was lying on his bed. It was still dark – perhaps not quite so dark. By the light of the dying fire he could see the clock: it was three o'clock. He looked round the room but could not see

Mickle. Why had he not yet returned? Michael was longing to ask hundreds of questions about the mysterious ceremony on the hill.

Far, far away he heard a cock crow in the darkness, and it was answered by another closer at hand.

'I wish morning would come,' Michael thought, and turned over in bed impatiently. As he did so such a violent wave of sickness and giddiness came over him that he almost toppled out of bed, and had to lie still a moment with heart pounding and sweat breaking out on his temples.

'I do feel queer,' he thought. 'Can I have eaten something that's made me sick?' After a few minutes he felt a little better, and had just decided that all was well when the feeling came back even worse than before.

He stood it for a little while, then struggled out of bed and put on a dressing-gown. Once before he had been troubled by frightful pains in the night, caused by unripe greengages, and Miss Simkin had given him a soothing draught. He tiptoed along the passages towards her room and very quietly opened the door. He was about to whisper 'Miss Simkin,' when he was startled by a low voice in the darkness, saying,

'What else have you learned?'

Michael remained silent, frozen, with his mouth open.

He heard Miss Simkin's voice reply.

'The King has given up his magic operations,' she said. 'He was making no headway. You have nothing to fear from him.'

'Go on.'

'I'm beginning to suspect that Prince Michael knows something.'

'What makes you think so?'

'He has been learning to talk animal language on the sly,' said the governess. 'He has been on a number of secret expeditions, some of them at night; he has been meddling with magic, and he's very thick with that cat of his, who knows a lot more than he pretends to, I'm sure.'

Michael's heart gave an uncomfortable bound at this. It was disconcerting to find the governess had been watching him so closely.

'It might be very inconvenient if he stumbled on any of our plans before we are ready.'

'Yes, yes,' said Miss Simkin eagerly. 'Anything likely to delay the glorious day would be *most* unfortunate.'

'Well,' said the voice impatiently, 'we can soon settle him. A hostage would be quite useful. We must take him to Down Under.'

'You mean ki-kidnap him?' she asked nervously.

'You must put him out of action – *and* the cat – and we'll come for them tonight.'

'Put him out of action? How?' Miss Simkin sounded

terrified. 'When I undertook Secret Service work for you it was on the understanding that there was to be no violence.'

'It's only drugging,' said the voice crossly. 'Here, take this drugged pad and, as soon as I've gone, nip along to the boy's room and put him under – hold it under his nose for two minutes. The cat sleeps on his bed, doesn't it? You can do them both at the same time. Lock them in a cupboard somewhere safe and we'll come for them tonight.'

Another wave of dizziness nearly overcame Michael. Clenching his knuckles, he backed through the door as silently as he had come, and flew back to his bedroom. His one thought was to warn Mickle. But Mickle still had not returned, unless he was in his own room. Michael went downstairs, but Mickle's room was empty.

He felt so bad that he sat down there, and must have fallen into a doze, for the next thing he heard was the stable clock striking six. He struggled to his feet and looked about in the dim light, but there was no sign of Mickle. His mouth was dry, his head throbbed, and he was as hot as fire.

He heard voices from the kitchen and thought with longing of tea; he would go and ask the kitchen staff for a cup and come back – that would take only a couple of minutes.

He staggered across the great Hall and through the baize-covered door into the servants' hall. A comforting murmur of chatter met his ears.

'You can't beat a good Indian, I say—'

'Earl Grey's my tipple—'

Mrs Epis the cook saw Michael and let out a shriek of dismay.

'Heart alive, you precious mite, whatever's the matter? You're as white as a dish towel!'

'May I have a cup of tea please?' said Michael hoarsely, and collapsed on to the floor in a dead faint.

There was consternation among the kitchen staff, but Mrs Epis soon had them in order.

'Put him on the sofa with a pillow and undo his collar. No, James, we do not want the King and Queen roused, nor the governess – what use would they be? I'd as soon have a yard and a half of wet fish. Glad, go and send a boy for Dr Bones, he's got more sense than that Lord Sweffling of Seal they have for the Queen's earache; and send for half a dozen nurses. Ethel, go and make up a bed for the Prince in the Isolation wing in case he's got anything catching, poor lamb, and light a fire. When you've done that, fetch all his night-clothes and handkerchiefs from his bedroom. Mr Wolfgang, if you will be so kind, just get out the second-best Madeira for the doctor. Rene, come and help me get his slippers off and have a look at his feet, we don't want the doctor to see him with toenails that will disgrace us. And, Glad, when you've sent the message, just pop the kettle on for another cup of tea; seeing the Prince like that has made me feel downright queer.'

The doctor's carriage arrived ten minutes later. Dr Bones examined Michael in a businesslike way, prodding so hard that he came out of his faint with a grunt of anguish. Looking round, he seemed to see a ring of faces all staring at him anxiously.

'Mickle – warn Mickle,' he muttered.

'Yes, my lovekin, don't worry. We'll look after your puss-cat.' That was Mrs Epis, warm and comforting. Then she turned to the doctor and added, 'He's delirious, poor moppet.'

Mickle returned to the Palace by way of Minerva's field.

He found her still asleep with her head hanging over the dewy grass.

'Did you have a successful evening?' she asked when he woke her.

'We learnt a lot. I'll just go in and make sure Michael got home safely – I had to send him on ahead because I had a duty call to pay – and then I'll come back and tell you. We have to start moving fast – things are going to begin happening any day now.'

He disappeared into the shrubbery and went lightly in at Michael's window. He was puzzled to find no Prince in the bed, and was still searching when the figure of Miss Simkin appeared from behind the window curtains, grabbed him by the scruff of the neck and thrust a drugged pad under his nose. She locked him into the nursery cupboard and took away the key.

The Prince, she decided, must have got up early and gone out, but there would be plenty of opportunity to drug him before the Under People returned.

11

Michael's next recollections were confused. At one moment he had been on a trolley, being wheeled along a narrow corridor between white walls. A cluster of lights above him had swum round and round like planets, and then, no time at all afterwards it seemed, his eyes were open and he was staring at a curtain, patterned all over with little pink and yellow flowers on wriggly black stems.

'Where's Mickle?' he said.

'Lawk alive, how the boy does go on. Don't ask me, duck. He'll turn up in his own good time, I daresay, whoever he is. Here, have a drink. Not too much, mind.'

After the drink, things became clearer. He saw that the pink and yellow flowers were on a screen, not a curtain; over the top of it he noticed two heads, turned away from him.

'Yes, very severe case of measles,' a voice said.

'Parents been told?'

'Gracious yes – bulletins every half-hour. Round this evening to see the boy ... Both had measles, fortunately.'

He dozed again. He was awakened presently by the door bursting open and a voice shouting, 'Hello, hello, hello! How's our cherub now?'

'Fine, thanks,' said Michael, opening his eyes and grinning weakly.

In fact he did feel a great deal better. The sickness and giddiness had gone, but, surveying himself in a mirror on the opposite wall, he saw that he was thickly covered with a vivid scarlet rash.

Facing him was a huge woman, broad as she was tall, in a blue starched dress all covered with medals, and a white cap like a ham-frill, with a large pink face under it. She strode to his bedside.

'Gave us a fright, you did!'

Michael felt rather foolish.

A terrified twitter came from a smaller white-capped head in the doorway,

'Matron! Matron! Here's her Majesty and his Majesty.'

'All right, show 'em up, show 'em up,' boomed the Matron. The King and Queen edged round the door, looking hardly less frightened, and the Matron bustled out.

'Father,' said Michael hurriedly, 'listen – Miss Simkin's a spy! She was going to kidnap me. She'll capture Mickle. You must arrest her.'

The King looked anxiously at the Queen, who said in a soothing voice,

'We couldn't quite do that, my lamb. She came on the very highest references from the Le Fays. But we'll keep on eye on Mickle, don't worry.'

'Can you have him brought here?'

'Oh, come, come, my boy, you're ill. Time enough for pets when you're better.'

'Well, may I see him please? Just for a few minutes?'

'Yes, yes,' the Queen said hurriedly. 'Now is there anything you'd like – orange-squash, grapes, books, hankies, games?'

'When shall I be allowed up?' said Michael eagerly.

'In a week, perhaps.'

A week! He did his best to conceal his horror, but his mind raced. Obviously it was no use trying to tell his parents anything; he would have to escape.

'I'd like some clothes and shoes to wear when I'm allowed up,' he said. 'And there's a tin of green gum in the school-room cupboard, I'd like that, please. It's nice to suck. And do *please* bring Mickle – I need to see him frightfully badly!'

Matron came rustling in. 'Time for mummies and daddies to say goodnight.'

The King and Queen rose with relief, kissed Michael and left the room. Michael heard the Queen say,

'Do you think he could still be delirious, Matron? He seemed to be talking oddly.'

'Ha, ha, yes, patients say some laughable things at times.'

'He was talking about a plot against his cat, he asked us to bring it here.'

The Matron's laugh boomed out.

'Yes, kiddies often want their pets; we have quite a lot of trouble. I should tell him the cat's lost for the moment.'

'As a matter of fact I haven't seen Mickle for a day or two,' the King said.

Next morning after breakfast Miss Simkin came to see Michael.

'Now, Miss Simkin, only ten minutes, please,' the Matron said. 'Nearly time for doctor's rounds.'

Michael gazed at Miss Simkin apprehensively. She seemed almost equally alarmed.

'We've been worried about you,' she said nervously. 'I was looking for you everywhere when I found you weren't in your room.'

I bet you were, Michael thought.

She had a large bundle with her.

'Here are some things her Majesty asked me to bring to you – trousers, shirt and shoes, I'll put them in this cupboard; a tin of green gum which looks *most* unwholesome; and your Father sent you a present.'

'Doctor's coming,' said Matron, putting her head in.

'I'm sorry I wasn't able to bring Mickle along,' Miss Simkin said; 'he was nowhere to be found.'

'I must see Mickle,' the Prince said, looking her in the eye. 'Please tell my Father that if he isn't brought by this afternoon I shall get up and look for him.'

Miss Simkin gave a sort of gasp and hurried out.

Meanwhile the Under Drug had not retained its effect on Mickle for very long. He soon began to struggle back to consciousness, and realized that he was imprisoned in the nursery cupboard. He wished, but nothing happened, and he found that his magic collar had been removed. Mickle was furious that he had let himself be taken so off his guard. Miss Simkin must be in the pay of the Under People; it was annoying that he had not guessed it. As soon as he heard footsteps approaching he crouched, ready to spring.

To his rage, Miss Simkin had anticipated this by wearing leather gloves. She grabbed him in mid-jump and stuffed him unceremoniously into a wicker basket with a lid, which was buckled down. Mickle hissed, more from anger than despair, and his rage and frustration increased tenfold on the long, jolting journey that followed. Miss Simkin walked, carrying the basket, for some distance, and then they seemed to be in a cart, for he heard the rumble of wheels and the rattle of hoofs. Much time passed, and then Miss Simkin picked up his basket again and he was lifted down.

Now he was being carried through woods: he could smell the sweet, damp scent of fallen leaves, and hear Miss Simkin shuffling through them. A couple of rabbits pattered, and a jay squawked.

At length Miss Simkin tapped on a door. Mickle was surprised that there should be a house in a wood; perhaps it was a keeper's hut. The door opened, he was picked up and taken inside.

A voice, the same soft voice he had heard once before in the library said,

'What is the meaning of this? Where is the other one?'

'There has been an unfortunate occurrence,' Miss Simkin replied. 'The boy has developed measles and is isolated in a wing of the Palace.'

'He must be captured none the less – as soon as possible. Borlock can keep an eye on him. You must go to his room tomorrow, drug him, and drop him (with due care) out of the window. We will arrange to have someone waiting to receive him. Meanwhile I'll keep this one here and question him.'

'You won't use unduly harsh methods?' she said.

'I shall use such methods as I consider suitable.'

Mickle disliked the sound of that.

He heard Miss Simkin walk towards the door. 'By the way, he was wearing this collar,' she said. 'I thought it was wiser to take it off.'

'You did well,' the voice said. Mickle heard the door shut. 'You can stay there tonight, my friend,' the voice went on.

'Twelve hours without food or water may put you in a help-ful frame of mind.'

Night came, and slowly, slowly, passed by. Next morning the lid was opened, and in a flash Mickle sprang out, but his captor was even quicker. A gauntleted hand grasped him by the scruff of the neck, and he was thrust into a bag which was tied so tightly round his throat that he almost choked, and left with his head sticking out. He glared at the person who had done this, and saw a man in a long black cloak.

'Who are you?' the man said, after staring at him.

Mickle made no reply.

'It will be better for you to answer my questions,' the man said. 'We are not patient with those who oppose us.'

Mickle still said nothing.

The man stood up. They were in a little wooden hut, with one small square window, high up, hanging from a hinge on the top. Mickle saw that the catch was unfastened and that the window swung to and fro slightly in the breeze. Then he noticed something more important – his collar, hanging over the back of the chair the man had been sitting on. If only he were not in the bag!

At this moment the man put him, bag and all, in a large basin.

'Now,' he said, 'if you don't answer my questions I'm going to fill this basin with water. Anything to say?'

Mickle stared at him with eyes like emerald sparks.

The water was icy, and made Mickle jump at its touch. The man poured it in slowly, so that it crept over his tail and hind legs, up his spine and front paws, till it reached his chin. He gave one fearful shudder, from top to toe, and flung himself sideways, tipping over the basin and spilling all the water.

The man swore, and grabbed him round the stomach. This had the lucky effect of pulling off the bag which had been loosened. Mickle bounded desperately forward and the man's hands slid off his soaked and slippery fur. A wet cat is one of the hardest things to hold. The chair was knocked over. Mickle heard his collar fall with a flop; he seized it in his teeth and it fastened itself round his neck.

'Take me out of here,' snapped Mickle. Instantly a strong pair of claws grasped him and he was whirled through the window and dropped outside.

Not knowing his whereabouts, he could not wish his way home. 'Take me down to those bushes,' he told the collar. They were as far as he could see. He bounded sideways into them just as his captor rushed furiously from the door of the hut. His leap carried him over the concealed lip of a quarry and he rolled helplessly down its slope, but at least he was out of sight. From the bottom of the quarry he could see a long glade, and a gate at the edge of the wood. He wished, and the claws carried him to the gate. Thank goodness, there, beyond it, was a farm he recognized. At last he knew where he was: at least thirty miles from home.

'I wish I was at the Palace,' he said in great relief, but nothing happened. Either his collar had gone wrong, or else he had used up his ration of wishes for twelve hours. His only comfort was that he had escaped from the man in black. Wet, weary, and discouraged, he sat down in the bushes to lick himself dry.

12

When Miss Simkin had gone, Michael called his nurse.

'Could you have a message sent to my parents?'

'Yes, love, I'll tell Matron,' she said. 'Something your governess forgot?'

'I want my father told that if Mickle is not sent here tomorrow I shall get up and go to look for him. And I mean that. It's the death penalty for anyone who lays violent hands on the Crown Prince,' said Michael, remembering an old law and trying to look very threatening, 'so people had better not try and stop me.'

The nurse looked alarmed and felt his pulse. Soon Matron flounced in and told him that he was an impertinent boy, but the doctor had said they supposed they must give in to his whims.

Next morning Miss Simkin appeared again, carrying a cat basket from which came a frenzied mewing.

'I'll just shut the window in case your puss makes a bolt for it,' said the nurse who accompanied Miss Simkin, and slid up the sash, leaving six inches open at the top. A large black cat jumped out of the basket – Michael could see at a glance that it was not Mickle – and darted angrily round the room.

Just then Michael heard Matron's loud, jolly laugh outside, and a man's voice with a foreign accent.

'Oh, here comes Matron with the specialist, Dr Subter,' said the nurse in alarm. 'We'd better pop Pussy back in the basket.'

Pussy was not anxious to be caught, and Matron put her head round the door while Miss Simkin was still chasing him.

'Oh, Miss Simkin,' she said affably, 'Dr Subter would like a word with you.'

'Quick,' Michael hissed to the cat, ignoring the nurse, 'while she's out of the room, tell me who you are?'

'I'm Blackie, from the Home Farm,' the cat answered aggrievedly. 'I was having a bit of a wash on the porch when she grabbed me and put me in that stuffy basket, don't ask me why.'

'Do you know where Mickle is?'

'Haven't seen him lately, I'm afraid. We move in rather different circles.'

'If you do see him, please tell him to beware of Miss Simkin, who is a kidnapper working with the enemy.'

'Is that so?' said Blackie with interest. 'In that case I fancy you'd better look out for yourself. I saw her talking in the orchard to Dr Subter, the man outside, and he said to her, "We'll easily deal with the child. Drug him, and put the black ointment on his rash, and I'll get him away."'

'Golly!' said Michael. 'Thank you. He must be in league with the Under People. You'd better escape through the window. Do warn Mickle if you can.'

He leaned across to the window, in spite of a scandalized exclamation from the nurse, and flung up the bottom sash.

'Thanks – I'll remember. Take care of yourself,' said Blackie, leaping out.

'Well! What ever did you do that for?' exclaimed the nurse.

'It was the wrong cat,' Michael explained. He saw Blackie settle down outside the window as if he thought Michael might be needing help, and then he had an idea.

'Nurse! Could you reach me the tin from my locker, the one with the green gum in it? And a glass of water? Thank you.'

'Don't drink too much,' she warned, going out of the door. The voices of Miss Simkin and the Matron came nearer. They ushered in a tall, pale man in a white jacket.

'Well, well,' he said. 'So this is my little patient. Don't bother to wait, Matron.' He smiled at Matron in a fasci-nating way that showed all his teeth, and she smiled back, quite melted, and then bustled out. The door closed, and Miss Simkin, as if absent-mindedly, pushed an armchair against it.

'You want to see his rash?' she said. 'Unbutton and show him, Michael.'

Michael obeyed slowly and reluctantly. The tall man spread a great deal of coal-black ointment on his chest. Michael did not like this, but reasoned that its purpose could not be harmful if they wanted him as a live hostage. Certainly the ointment had a wonderfully soothing effect, and seemed to take away all the itchiness.

Suddenly there was a sickly smell, and he saw Miss Simkin's hand, holding a handkerchief, sliding up towards his face. Quick as lightning he snatched it from her, taking her by surprise, and flung it out through the open window.

'Oh you little brat!' she exclaimed.

'Go out and get it,' said the doctor calmly. 'It's in that bush.' Miss Simkin moved the armchair and darted out of the door, giving Michael a furious look. In a minute she appeared outside, searching among the bushes. Michael heard her give a cry of rage, and he saw the noble Blackie tear past with something white in his mouth.

'That cat's gone off with it,' she gasped. Dr Subter moved to the window.

Michael glanced down at his hands. When would his rash act of swallowing the Diatherma block take effect? To his delight he saw that his fingers had already vanished. As he looked his hands disappeared and his arms melted away up to the shoulders. By squinting slightly he was just able to see his nose go.

Dr Subter turned back and uttered an oath. He began feverishly searching the room, looking behind the screen, under the bed, in the cupboard. While he did this Michael rolled out and got under the bed, as he was not intangible.

Miss Simkin came back. 'That cat dropped it in the pond,' she said furiously. Dr Subter whirled on her.

'The accursed boy has vanished now, thanks to your bungling,' he said viciously. She looked incredulously about the room and ran out into the passage, exclaiming, 'He can't have gone far.'

The doctor followed her.

Michael grabbed his clothes and possessions, and slipped out after them. The black ointment had done him a lot of good, and this seemed a splendid chance to escape. He went into the bathroom next door and dressed – not an easy process, as he could not always find his arms and legs. Then he made his way quietly downstairs.

Seeing the Matron in the corridor with Dr Bones he had an inspiration and called out, in a fairly good imitation of his nurse's voice,

'Matron! Matron, come quickly, they're kidnapping

Prince Michael – the governess and the foreign doctor! They're drugging him.'

The Matron looked startled and ran along the corridor. She was followed by Dr Bones and several nurses.

Halfway along they met Miss Simkin and Dr Subter opening all the doors and looking through them.

'What are you doing? Where is Prince Michael?' demanded the Matron.

'We've lost him – I mean, he's vanished.'

'Nonsense! A child can't just vanish. Where's the nurse who called me?'

Michael crept up behind Dr Subter and put an invisible hand in his pocket, hoping to find something incriminating. To his delight he drew out two things of unfamiliar pattern but unmistakable use – a gag and a small dagger. He dropped them on the floor with a clatter. The results were most satisfactory. Dr Subter swore, and stooped to pick them up, but it was too late.

'Look,' said Dr Bones, 'what's he got those for?'

'That nurse was speaking the truth,' cried the Matron. 'What have you done with the child?'

Dr Subter saw that he was in a tight place; he prudently vanished, leaving Miss Simkin to face the wrath of the medical attendants and to swear vainly that she had not touched a hair of Michael's head and did not know where he was. The foreign specialist's mysterious disappearance was the last straw, and she was denounced as a witch, a kidnapper, and a spy, and locked in the linen cupboard until she could be taken to the police station and charged with high treason.

Michael walked out of the Palace with the happy feeling that something useful had been accomplished, and went round to Minerva's field.

'Hey!' he called from a distance.

She raised her head from her grazing and looked searchingly in his direction.

'Is that you, Michael? Where are you?'

'I'm over here, invisible.'

'Oh, that old trick,' she said indulgently. 'Come over, but not too fast – let me hear where you put your feet. I'm too old for hide and seek.'

He coughed when he was beside her, and laid a hand on her neck.

'I thought you were ill?' she said.

'I was, but I'm better now.' He was surprised to find that this was nearly true. That Under-ointment must have been potent stuff. He told Minerva his story and she nodded her head slowly up and down.

'I never did like that governess,' she said. 'I hope they put her in prison. But it's serious about Mickle – it looks as if they must have got him.'

'Miss Simkin had the whole of yesterday to get him away,'

said Michael miserably. 'He's probably in Down Under by now.'

He pondered for a while. 'I think,' he said at last, 'that I'd better try and get into Down Under. I must rescue Mickle, and I may be able to find the magic box; now we know all we're likely to find out I shouldn't wait any longer.'

He expected an outburst of protests from Minerva, but to his surprise she said, 'I think you are right. I'll take you to the cave. Hop off and get what you need and we'll start before it's dark. Shouldn't you leave a note for your father, telling him not to worry?'

'Yes, I'll do that,' said Michael, and ran off, glad to have a definite plan.

While he was packing some food and spare socks and a compass in a bag he took out of his pocket the package that his father had sent him when he was ill. He undid it and found a little flexible piece of tubing made of hard, green-ish stuff. When he put it in the bag it lit up the inside.

'Of course, it's my grandfather's invention, the luminous torch that father was talking about,' he thought. 'It lasts forty-eight hours. Just the thing for Down Under.'

He wrote a note to his father, saying that he was quite all right but had been called away on urgent State business, that he would be back soon and they were not to worry. Then he spent half an hour on a fruitless search for Mickle, but at last returned to Minerva.

'I don't like your going off on your own like this,' she said as they cantered along the familiar route. 'But at least you're invisible, and you owe it to Mickle to try and find him. I'd come with you, but I should be useless underground in caves – they'd hear me coming miles off.'

'No, you must stay up here,' Michael said, 'and keep an eye on things. I'll try and get messages back somehow.'

'And don't go messing about with magic,' she said earnestly, 'I'm sure no good can come of it. You speak animal language, that's a useful talent – make the most of it. There are sure to be some animals down there and any animal will help you, they're much more trustworthy than humans.'

Michael dismounted at the cave entrance and gave her a hug.

'Don't wait; go straight back,' he said. 'If I do manage to send anyone with a message I'll tell them to go to your field. Don't worry, I'll be back as soon as I can, with Mickle, I hope.'

She nodded, turned, and cantered off.

Once in her field she very sensibly went to sleep. The situation was distressing: both her friends were in danger, and the kingdom might be attacked at any moment, but it was certain that staying awake all night would not help matters, so she slept.

Five minutes after midnight Mickle, whirling to earth in

a dragon-chariot, found her sleeping in the moonlight and woke her.

'Has he found you already?' she said in astonishment.

'Who? I've only just got back – I was kidnapped. Where's Michael? Is it true that he's ill?'

'He was—' Minerva began. She stopped, overcome by horror as she realized what had happened.

'Well, what? Where is he now?'

'He thought you must have been taken to Down Under, and he's gone off there to look for you.'

'Through the cave mouth? By himself? *Minerva*, how could you let him go? When did he leave? I must go after him.'

'He went hours ago. Before it was dark. You'd never catch up with him now – besides he's invisible, even you could hardly find an invisible boy in a dark city.'

'No, there's not much chance. None really,' Mickle said hopelessly.

'We must wait until we hear from Michael,' Minerva's tone was decisive. 'But in the meantime we can rouse the kingdom.'

By the next day there was alarm and dismay in the Palace. Michael's note had been found and taken to the King, who did not believe it; he was in such a state of mind that he was not even sure if it was Michael's own handwriting, but if it was, it had probably been written under compulsion. He could think of nothing but that moment when the magic talking machine prophesied:

'Your son will go alone among them.'

At last in despair he resolved to try the machine again, but all it would say was, 'Your enemies are nearer than you think.' As it had always said that his enemies were all about him, the King was hardly enlightened by this news.

'If only I knew what they were going to do,' he

muttered, 'or where they were going to come from. It's no use mobilizing the army. It would only be in the wrong place.'

He ran his hands through his hair and sank into dejection.

13

Michael hesitated for a moment in the mouth of the cave. Should he, after all, have told his father what he planned to do? But that would only have meant delay and opposition. The main thing, he thought, was to get into Down Under, rescue Mickle, and steal the magic box. Somehow he felt sure that it would solve all their problems.

He had enough food for several days. After that he would have to rely on luck.

He went forward into the sandy passage, which ran straight ahead for a little way and then turned at right angles. It was fairly wide and high; he could walk without stooping. Soon it began to go downhill steeply and became rather damp. The walls changed from sandstone to rock, which dripped reddish water. A few drops from the ceiling fell on him. He thought he must be under the swamp.

He walked carefully, with one hand on the rock wall and the other holding his luminous torch. Now as he walked he began to hear a dull thud, thud, thud, which made the ground tremble under his feet. Could the Underground people be blasting or mining, or boring a way to the outside world? At every turn he half expected to see black figures ahead of him in the gloom hammering at the rock.

Unconsciously he began to hurry, and soon the thud changed to a muffled booming, which increased to a roar.

'Of course,' he said, 'I know what it is, it's the waterfall. The passage is making straight for it. What a fool I am.' He pressed on.

Finally the deafening roar seemed to be all round him, and water came down in solid sheets from the roof; he must be right under the fall.

Wiping the water from his eyes, he saw two openings in the wall ahead on his left, and looked into them. To his disappointment they went only a few feet into the wall. He wondered what they could be, and finally decided that they must have been made by Giles and his party in one of their attempts to bore their way out.

Then another thought struck him. How queer it was that they hadn't found the passage by which he had come! Surely it was obvious enough? He turned to look, and realized that actually it was not at all obvious. His passage led round a projecting bump of rock, over which water fell in sheets, spouting to the ground and splashing up. Unless you looked very carefully you would never have noticed that there was a narrow dark opening beside the rock, so completely was it veiled by the water.

Michael disliked what he had heard of the Underground people, but he felt sorry for them just then. It seemed dreadful that they must have been as close as that to the way out and never knew it.

The passage brought him to a little square cave with a shelf in the rock at one side. He thought it must be the room where the treasure had been left, and hunted for traces. He found some candle-ends and what might have been the buckle of an old-fashioned shoe. Then he looked for the way which he knew must lead on towards Down Under, and discovered it at last, high up in the wall. He had a good deal of difficulty in climbing up to it. The cave in which he came out was larger than the first and narrowed at one end into a crevice. Across this crevice ran a stream which disappeared under a low arch in the rock.

'Well, if they went under the arch with the treasure,' he thought, 'I suppose I can do it with my pack.'

It was the most uncomfortable journey he had ever made. He had to go along bending double, up to his knees in water. He had walked perhaps a hundred yards like this when he saw something red flash in the water at his foot. He stooped and picked it up.

As he crouched, gazing at the thing in his hand, long-forgotten words came back to him, the words of a jingle his old nurse used to sing to him:

> *A dragon-red heart inside a crown*
> *On Astalon's long-lost sceptre-stone.*

He was holding a ruby the size of a walnut, and on it was engraved a heart in a crown. It was sure proof that the treasure-stealers had passed this way. He pocketed it, and struggled on.

Presently his right hand met the edge of a shelf or cranny in the wall. He resolved to try crawling along it, but soon wondered if he had made the wrong decision, for the crawl-ing was even more difficult than stooping, owing to the lowness of the roof. Just as he was becoming so tired that it seemed impossible to move any more, the shelf widened a little and the roof became high enough for him to walk beside the stream. He now discovered a small but dry cave and here, without troubling much about whether he was still invisible, he dropped down with his head on the pack and slept.

When he woke – and he had no idea how long he had been asleep – he ate some of his provisions, and consulted his torch. It was still perfectly bright, so he could not have been underground for forty-eight hours yet.

He started off once more. The going was easy enough now, and he found that the tunnel was becoming wider and higher all the time. After an hour or so's walking he saw a faint light ahead, which grew brighter, and by degrees he could distinguish black shapes, the buildings Brock had spoken about, with shafts of light coming down between them. They seemed to tower miles above his head.

All his confidence deserted him. He crept forward step by step. As he halted beside a jagged outcrop of rock the lights suddenly went out. What should he do? He decided to wait until they lit up again, for he would be at a greater advantage over the inhabitants in light than in darkness.

He did not have to wait long. Evidently the people of Down Under had a brief spell of dark from time to time – perhaps to soothe their eyes. When the great beams shone down again he walked swiftly on towards the shadows of the city which ran out to meet him. As he passed between two of the rock buildings he saw with a cold clutch at his heart that some people were coming towards him.

Luckily his invisibility was still sufficient, and they passed by without seeing him. Behind him he heard them talking to each other in a strange guttural language, a little like Brock.

He saw a turning on his left, a narrow alley. He followed it, and came out into a great square, or courtyard. On the opposite side of it were lower buildings, resembling sheds or barns. He stood in the shadows, wondering whether to cross the square.

A door opened, on the side facing him, and a crowd of men poured out. They drew up into formation and stood still. Soon four men in black and silver appeared and strolled along, apparently inspecting them. One of the four shouted a command.

The soldiers (for such Michael guessed them to be) pulled out blue-flashing swords and engaged in some complicated fencing exercises. Michael thought the swords must be magic for if a soldier was touched by another man's sword he fell to the ground as though he were dead, but recovered after ten minutes or so. The swords seemed to produce a temporary shock or stunning effect.

Presently the swordplay came to an end, and some piercingly shrill music began, played on instruments like fifes.

The men all ran to one side of the square, and Michael could hear a curious rustling, in the intervals of the fife music. A huge pair of double doors was pushed back, and out of them came seething – what? For an instant Michael thought it was men crawling on their stomachs, then with horror he decided that it must be snakes, about the size and thickness of humans. The whole middle part of the square filled with them in a couple of minutes, wriggling, writhing, knotting and un-knotting like something out of a nightmare.

Michael gasped with admiration as the men ran forward and each seized a snake. They seemed to have their own, which they approached unerringly. The creatures were harnessed and bridled, packs were fastened to their backs, and they were drawn up tidily in formation.

'They can't be poisonous, surely,' he thought. 'But who'd have imagined you could sort out that lot so quickly. Do they use the snakes for transport, I wonder?'

At that moment he heard a kind of stifled sobbing near him, and a voice complaining miserably to itself.

'Reef? That's no reef. Might be a timber-hitch or a blackwall-hitch, but, whatever it is, may I be turned into a slow-worm if I can get it undone.' The language it spoke was not unlike Basic Fish.

Michael turned cautiously and saw one of the snakelike creatures near him. It had got its tail tangled up into an

123

enormous and inextricable knot, and was weeping quietly as it tried in vain to undo itself.

The impulse to snatch a knot away from somebody and have a go at it is irresistible. 'Here, let me try,' said Michael in Basic Fish, and he began levering at the knot.

'Oh, I *am* so obliged,' sighed the creature, letting both its ends go limp. At close quarters Michael could see that it was brownish-pink, and formed all of rings from top to toe. Top and toe were exactly the same.

'Are you a snake?' Michael asked, hauling away at a yielding loop.

'Certainly not,' it said haughtily, 'I'm *lumbricius terrestris*, a highly superior earthworm.'

'Oh that's why you look so familiar. You've certainly got yourself in a tangle.'

'It's being so big,' the worm said sadly. 'My human attendant's ill, and there's no one to keep me unsnarled. Oh, thank you, thank you—' as the last end was tugged through the last loop, 'dear me, now it's *much* easier to breathe. I hope I can do you a return service some time. Just whistle when you want me; the name's Glob.' It wreathed itself affectionately round Michael's legs.

'Don't get knotted again.'

'No, all is well now,' said the worm happily. 'Adieu, kind friend.'

At this moment a heavy hand fell on Michael's shoulder.

Impeded by the friendly Glob, he could not escape. He realized with dismay that the effects of the Diatherma had worn off, and, though thin and patchy, he was plainly visible! If only he had stayed in the shadow, instead of stepping forward to help the worm! Two of the soldiers had grabbed him, and now one held his arms pinioned behind his back while the other took his pack to the officer, who looked sharply at its contents and hurried towards the passage through which Michael had come, shouting an order as he went. Michael was marched after him, under a guard of six men. There was no possible chance of escape.

As they left the square he caught a tantalizing glimpse of creatures filing out that resembled huge ants, wearing harness and saddle-bags. It seemed the Under People must have invented a process for enormously increasing the size of such insects.

'I'd hate to be bitten by an ant that size,' he thought.

He was marched to a large building with a massive square porch, all carved out of black rock, and jostled along a pitch-dark passage. Already his first terror was wearing off, but he was very miserable, and cursed himself again and again for his carelessness.

One of his escorts tapped at a door. It swung open, letting out a beam of dazzling light. Michael staggered blindly forward, at a shove from one of the soldiers, and the door closed behind him.

When his eyes became accustomed to the brightness he saw that he was in an office or military headquarters. Maps hung on the walls, several of them recognizable as parts of Astalon. The officer who had brought him was there. 'This is the captive, Commander,' he said.

Sitting at the desk, looking at Michael intently, was a man in a black cloak.

'Well,' said this man, 'who are you?' Michael could understand him well enough, but he did not answer.

The Commander began turning over some things on his desk, which Michael saw were the contents of his pack. He was glad the torch was still in his pocket. There was a little food, his compass, a pocket-knife, and his notebook, which the man proceeded to examine.

'He won't find much to help him in that,' Michael thought, grinning in spite of himself as he remembered the names of butterflies and wildflowers all mixed up with square roots and birthdays in its pages. While the man studied these, Michael looked at the maps on the walls. One was extremely clear – a map of the country lying between the Palace and Dingle Warren. There was a large black square marked First Entrance, a smaller one marked Second Entrance, and three lines of dots with arrow heads leading towards the Palace, and marked First, Second, and Third Lines of Attack. Michael shivered. It was obvious that the attack was coming very soon.

Putting the notebook on one side, the Commander picked up the compass, and pressed the catch down to open it. Not till that moment did Michael remember with a sinking of the heart that the words 'Michael' and 'Astalon' were engraved inside the lid, with a crown and a P. His father had given it to him on his last birthday.

'H'm,' said the Commander at length, 'so that's who you are, is it? I expected as much.' Michael wondered why he was so little surprised. The officer murmured a question.

'Borlock,' the Commander answered in a low voice. 'He prophesied last year that some wretched prince would come spying about. We'd better go and see him; he'll want to get his Insight to work on this. Lock the door and leave the guard outside.' Both men went out hurriedly, leaving Michael alone.

Presently he heard a faint squeak, and a fluttering behind him. He jumped slightly, and looked round. High up on the wall in a metal cage something dark was flapping about. He heard a tiny voice like that of Nicodemus, but even shriller, crying, 'Let me out! Let me out! Let me out!'

'Who are you?' asked Michael, trying to make out what sort of creature it was. He saw a pair of bright eyes.

'I'm a bat,' it said. 'You're not an Under-boy, are you? They don't speak U.A.L.'

'No I'm not,' Michael answered. 'Why are you in a cage?'

'They keep us as pets. Do let me out! I was caught yesterday and I can't stand it. I shall go mad in this cage.'

'All right,' said Michael, glancing round to make sure no
one was likely to come in.

He climbed on a high stool and unlatched the cage. The
bat flopped out, circled the room, making him duck, and
came to rest upside down on a framed map.

'Thanks,' it said. 'Now if you could open the window I'll
flap off before anyone comes. Anything I can do for you in
return?'

'Well—' said Michael, 'I don't know if you could. I do
want someone to carry a message to the Upper World.'

'Yes, yes, I can easily do that,' squeaked the bat. 'We bats
have several crannies and crevices in the roof. I often nip
out at night.'

'Can you contact a horse called Minerva who lives in one
of the paddocks of the Royal Palace of Astalon?' said
Michael tearing a piece of paper from a sandwich-wrapping
and hurriedly scribbling. 'Now then, how can I tie this on
you?'

The bat cautiously sidled up to him. Feeling in his pocket
for some string to strap the message on its body, he found
the Astalon ruby, and, on impulse, folded it inside his letter.
He did not much care for the feel of the bat; it was cold and
furry and spiny. He wondered if he was wise to trust it.

He heard steps coming along the passage, so he quickly

opened the window and threw out the bat, which performed a graceful wheel in salute, squeaked a final word of gratitude, and vanished upwards.

The officer came in and looked at Michael suspiciously.

'No use jumping out of that window, my young friend,' he said. 'It's a long drop to the street.'

Presently the man in the black cloak returned, and said, 'He's to go to Borlock at once.'

14

Mickle prowled about the Palace uneasily. He learned that Miss Simkin was in prison, which was satisfactory. The King was in a state of collapse, and kept sending messages to the Commander-in-Chief of the Army, and then rescinding them. Mickle impatiently decided to go and have another consultation with Minerva.

As he strolled across the lawn he noticed a great commotion in the sky over her paddock. A huge swarm of rooks, all talking at once, were circling round Minerva, rising and falling like large black gnats.

Minerva was looking a little confused.

'Can I be of any assistance?' asked Mickle courteously, as he came up.

'Oh, I'm so glad you've come,' she sighed with relief. 'These rooks have brought a bat who says he has a message, but it's strapped to his stomach, and *I* can't get it off, and I don't want them to try – they'd probably tear it to pieces among them, bat and all.'

'Caw, ma'am, how could such a gawgeous piece of hawsflesh be so hawty?' said Lord Porty, the leader rook, bobbing up impudently under Minerva's nose. 'We brawt the little feller-me-lad, didn't we, boys? Chawnced on him flittin' around, all lost and lonesome, with a letter tucked in his cummerbund, and I said, "Boys, you don't often see bats bearing billay-duckses, let's have a dekko at this one," and caw, stone the crows if it hasn't got a crown on it. He says "Can you direct me to the Royal Palace?" so we gave him a fawmal escawt, with a twenty-one caw salute.' Here all the rooks started cawing until no one could hear themselves think.

'Very kind of you,' said Mickle politely when the racket died down. 'Now perhaps you'll be so good as to clear off a little and give us some space, as you seem to be frightening the messenger.'

The rooks burst into shrieks of derisive laughter at this, for the poor little bat, on seeing a large black cat coming to remove his letter, had nearly fainted with fright. Mickle delicately removed the letter with one claw, unfolded it, and read it to Minerva.

'Am a prisoner in Down Under, but all right. Attack imminent from Dingle Warren – warn Father and mobilize army. No sign of Mickle. They have magic swords, giant ants, and racing worms. I'll try to send more messages. This is the Astalon sceptre stone. Michael P.'

'We must take that to the King at once,' said Minerva. 'You speak to him, Mickle, you can talk human speech when you want to, and we'll all come, to convince him it's serious.'

The rooks were delighted at the idea of being a delegation, and rioted up to the Palace, looping the loop and making fun of the quiet little bat who flitted sedately among them. Minerva followed with Mickle, who tucked the letter and ruby into his collar.

Mickle went into the Palace and found the King in the East Drawing-room. He beckoned the delegation to the terrace outside the french window.

The King was sitting hunched miserably over the fire with his head in his hands.

'Your Majesty!' said Mickle sharply.

The King jumped and looked round.

'Who's there?' he said trembling.

'I'm here,' Mickle replied patiently. 'I have a message for you from the Prince,' and he took out the folded paper.

'I'm dreaming, I suppose,' said the King, reading it absently. 'I never knew I had such a powerful imagination. Talking cats ... messages ... I just don't believe it.' He slumped back in his chair and was about to toss the paper into the fire when Mickle jumped up and bit his hand, rather severely.

The King let out a yell, which brought Queen Elfrida hurrying from the next room.

'What is it, dear?'

'That cat bit me.'

'Is that all?'

'It's not all,' said Mickle, very crossly. 'I have an important message from Prince Michael, and the King persists in thinking it's only a dream. Will you please convince him it is not? The rest of the delegation is waiting outside the window, if you'd be so kind as to open it.'

The Queen went rather white, but opened the window composedly enough. Minerva stepped through, followed by the rooks and the bat, who settled on the chandeliers. At sight of them, the poor King's overworked nervous system gave way entirely, and with a shriek he fainted dead away.

'You should burn feathers under his nose,' Mickle suggested.

Two of the rooks obligingly dropped some.

'Never mind him for the moment,' said the Queen who was reading the note. 'This is certainly Michael's handwriting,' she said to Mickle. 'Where did it come from?'

'The bat brought it. Michael gave it to him in Down Under.'

'And why, pray, are all these other creatures here?'

'They came to see the note safely delivered.'

'And why did you never tell us that you could speak human language?'

'Because I didn't want to be bothered with a lot of unnecessary questions,' Mickle said coldly.

'Oh. Well I'm very much obliged to you for bringing the message,' the Queen said, unbending a little. 'Where is the sceptre stone, by the way?' Mickle showed it to her and she nodded. 'Yes, that is undoubtedly genuine. You had better give it to the King; it is a stone of power. Wait a minute,' she added, as the delegation turned to leave, and she opened a silver biscuit barrel on a side table. She gave them each a pink, sugar-topped biscuit. The rooks cawed gratefully over theirs, but Mickle gave his to Minerva as soon as they were outside, and the little bat, after sniffing his in a puzzled way, passed it to Lord Porty.

'Ta very much I'm shaw,' said the rook and swallowed it whole. 'Want us to see you home, Batty? Okeydoke, no trouble.'

'Just a minute, Bat,' said Minerva. 'If you should see the Prince again, tell him his message has been delivered, and give him this.' She passed him a hair from her mane.

'Ta-ta,' shouted the rooks, and swung off with the bat in their midst.

Mickle glanced back through the window. The Queen had summoned a messenger and was writing a note to the Chief of Staff. That done, she picked up two of the rooks' feathers, held them in the fire a moment, and put them, all smoking and sizzling, under the King's nose.

'Good,' said Mickle, 'I put more reliance in her than in his Majesty.'

'You never gave him the ruby,' Minerva said accusingly.

Mickle grinned.

'If it's a stone of power it's safer with me than with him.'

15

Michael had expected that the great magician would be living in some palace, but the guard left the city and took him through the huge cave and along the river.

'Borlock has a little house in the shadows,' one of them explained. 'He says that noise disturbs his experiments. Upsets the vibrations, or something.'

'What is he like?' Michael asked.

'He'll turn you inside out,' they told him, 'and find out things you didn't know yourself that you knew.'

Michael began to be rather anxious. He realized that he was still not quite well; his head ached and he felt tired and unable to face more questioning.

They came at last to a small dark building right up against the rock wall of the cave, about two miles from the city, and waited while the leader of the guard rapped on the door. Eventually it opened, very slowly and reluctantly, and an old, bearded face looked through the crack.

'Go away,' it said angrily. 'How many times do I have to tell you that I am not to be disturbed? What are you waiting for? Go away, I tell you.'

'But it's the prisoner for you to interrogate, sir.'

'Prisoner? What prisoner? Oh, the *prisoner*,' said Borlock. 'Why didn't you say so? Well, hand him over, and for goodness' sake take yourselves off, don't stand there like a lot of dummies.'

'Can you manage him, sir?'

'That little sprat? Don't insult me,' Borlock said, and sticking out a long skinny hand he grabbed Michael and pulled him inside. He pushed Michael along a passage and down some steps; a door opened ahead and he stumbled forward into a dim blue light. Borlock followed him.

They were in the wise man's study; Michael looked round him with interest. The walls were covered with glass-fronted shelves holding books, skeletons, test tubes, dried plants, and so forth. Complicated apparatus stood on tables, and there was a large, mysterious machine in one corner of the room. A pair of yellow eyes glared at Michael from near the ceiling; it was a large owl, seated on the top of a cupboard.

'Stand there,' said Borlock sharply, and pointed to a circle drawn in chalk on the floor. Michael stepped into it, feeling as if he were at the dentist's. Borlock sat down, looking at him with eyes like gimlets, and began to wave his hands up and down, humming monotonously under his breath. He looked extraordinarily odd, and Michael felt like giggling.

At last the humming stopped. Michael tried to move, but he seemed to be fastened to the ground, and could not even raise a finger. Borlock had cast a spell to prevent his getting away or being troublesome. He now examined Michael, muttered something in which the word 'pain' was audible, and began touching him here and there. When his hand fell on Michael's forehead, Michael could not wince or speak, but his eyes opened wider; Borlock nodded to himself and picked up a little glowing metal rod.

He touched Michael's head with the rod. Michael immediately felt wonderful relief from pain; his headache vanished never to return. Borlock now looked him over, saw that he was firmly fixed, smiled grimly, opened a large book, and instantly forgot Michael. He leaned his elbow on the table, pushed his beard into a more comfortable position and brooded.

Although Michael's limbs were powerless, his eyes were not, and he stared about the room as far as he see. There was a square thing covered with a cloth which interested him greatly, but it was to the side of him and he could only see it out of the corner of his eye.

Borlock was reading a book called *Permutations and*

Combinations. The title conveyed nothing to Michael, but he could see the book was full of columns of figures. Borlock was frowning furiously over it as if he loathed it. After a long period of study he put it on one side and started towards the square thing under the cover. Michael nearly burst with interest, but unfortunately Borlock suddenly caught his eye and stopped short.

'Oh, you're there, are you?' he said. 'Well, I don't suppose I shall get anything useful out of *you*.'

He pulled Michael's notebook towards him and looked at it crossly.

'Nothing here,' he said in disappointment. 'Moths, orchids – wait, what's this?'

On the back page Michael had written some figures in columns.

$$8.12$$
$$23.7$$
$$2.9$$
$$1.4$$

'What are they?' said Borlock, sticking out his head like a tortoise, and staring fiercely at Michael. Michael rolled his eyes, but could not utter a word.

'Stupid of me,' Borlock muttered, and touched Michael's lips lightly with a staff.

'It's a list of birthdays,' Michael said. 'My father's and mother's and mine, and my cat's. We don't know when his birthday is, so we pretend it's the first of April.'

'I'm not sure that I believe that,' said Borlock doubtfully. He copied out the figures, growled to himself, and finally approached Michael very close, stuck his face forward, and said:

'Name?'

'Michael.'

'Are you the Crown Prince of Astalon?'

'Yes I am.'

'Age? Birthplace? Hour of birth?' Michael gave them, feeling as if he were going in for an examination, and Borlock rapidly cast his horoscope, snorted over it, and threw it on one side.

'It says nothing,' he muttered. 'Have you a Significant Number?'

'Not that I know of,' said Michael, who had never heard of them.

'Don't be foolish, child,' exclaimed Borlock impatiently. 'If you have one, you know it.'

'Then I haven't one,' said Michael.

Fortunately the spell on Michael prevented all feelings of weariness, hunger, or thirst, for the magician soon forgot him again and went back to his calculations. This time they lasted for several days, as far as Michael could judge. From time to time Michael dozed, and always woke to see the old man working over his huge book.

Once there came a thunderous knock on the door and a voice shouted:

'Twelve o'clock, U-Day minus one.'

Michael was appalled by this. Could U-Day mean Upstairs Day, and was the invasion of Astalon about to begin? It sounded dreadfully like it. Borlock started at the interruption and threw his book on the floor.

'Perdition take them!' he cried. 'Why can't they leave me in peace?'

He cast his glittering glare round the room like a caged lion. Then he sprang up and began pacing backwards and forwards. Michael instinctively tried to shrink back each time Borlock passed him, but his muscles refused to obey.

'I've had enough of this so-called scientific method,' muttered Borlock savagely. 'Permutations and combinations – where do they get you? I've been working on this box for fifty years now – fifty years of my life wasted, and all for nothing. Let's try a bit of incantation for a change.'

He seized a little jar of blue ointment which he warmed over a candle flame and began rubbing over his face and hands. The effect was very sinister – the blueness accentuated his drawn, dangerous expression, and his lean blue hands waving to and fro looked more than ever like claws.

The ointment had a pungent scent, and began to give off a thread of smoke.

Borlock began reciting spells or runes in a low chant.

Michael had for some time been eyeing the magic staff which lay on a shelf near his head. He was longing to get hold of it. His hands were useless, but since Borlock had freed his lips his head was not quite so firmly fixed as the rest of him. He worked his mouth round, as if he was trying to loosen a bit of toffee from a tooth, and found that he could move his head just a fraction, if he exercised every ounce of will. He pushed out his lips to their fullest extent and found he could just touch the tip of the staff. By moving his lips up and down he managed to roll it towards him. He tried to grab it in his teeth, but to his bitter disappointment it rolled off the shelf and fell on the floor.

Borlock was too engrossed in his incantations to notice.

Michael gazed down despondently at the staff, which was now totally out of reach, six inches from his foot. As he looked at it, however, he began to feel a glowing, burning sensation in his lips and tongue, which spread slowly down his throat, up his nose and back inside his head.

It was like the prickling that follows an attack of pins and needles. It extended down to his stomach and along his legs and arms. Suddenly he realized that he was coming out of the spell. He could move his head now, and he cautiously turned it to see what Borlock was doing.

The sight filled him with excitement. The magician had taken the cloth off the square object and revealed it as a solid, polished box, made of black metal and engraved with symbols. On top of the box was a revolving dial, with holes. Borlock, who had become very thin, almost transparent, with all his spell-casting, was standing by the box, swaying to and fro, and dialling combinations of letters with inconceivable rapidity. Michael counted six, and then a pause, six, and then a pause, six, and then a pause.

'I know!' he thought, a light breaking in on him. 'What a clever man the Old King was. It's a combination lock, and that's why no one can open it, because they can't find the right combination of letters. Borlock's been trying to do it by mathematics for fifty years, using every possible combination from AAAAAA on, and now he's given that up and is using magic. I should think magic would be better.'

Borlock's present method, however, did not seem to be yielding any results, though he dialled combinations fast as flashes of light. The air round him was positively sulphurous. Michael crept forward, step by step, until he was almost looking over Borlock's shoulder. By this time the old man was hardly to be seen at all – there was nothing left of him but a spiral in the air tapering down to one skinny blue finger which twirled and twirled the silver dial.

The atmosphere was so thick with sulphur and magic and

tension that Michael could not restrain a sneeze. Borlock spun round and stood regarding him formidably.

'So!' he said. 'A clever boy. Here we have a visitor who, without asking, unlocks his little cage and steps out to watch things that are no concern of his. A very talented visitor. But wait—'

He made a rapid sideways movement. Michael guessed what he was after and hastily jumped back, putting his foot on the magic staff. With his eyes on Borlock he stooped, felt for it with his hand and picked it up.

'Very talented indeed – most bold and resourceful,' said Borlock silkily.

'And now I suppose you think, my young friend, that having command of the wand you are entitled to have a try at the combination? I suppose you think you are the one destined by fate to open the box. Yes?' and he suddenly thrust his face close to Michael's.

'Yes I do want to try it,' said Michael boldly. 'Why not? After all, my great-grandfather made it.'

'He wants to try,' said Borlock broodingly. 'Here have I been working on it for fifty years, and along comes young Whipper-Snapper and thinks he can open it at the first twiddle. The impertinence of it – the sheer, devilish, cross-grained impertinence of it.'

He was pacing to and fro, and Michael had very strongly the feeling that here was a man half mad with rage and disappointment – a very dangerous man who, driven to frenzy by frustration, might do some fatal deed. He wondered how the magician could be calmed down.

'Borlock,' he said hesitantly, 'I *would* like to try, but I expect it's no use dialling something obvious like Astalon or Open Sesame, because you're sure to have tried everything like that long ago, aren't you?'

'He wants to pick my brains now,' snarled Borlock. 'Well, I don't mind telling you that I've tried every six-letter word in English, French, all the European, Scandinavian, Slavonic, Asian, African, and Polynesian languages, not to mention Greek, Latin, Hebrew, Sanskrit, and all languages not now in use, and if that helps you at all, you're welcome to it. And let me tell you, too—' he added as Michael took an irresistible step towards the box, 'if you so much as lay a finger on that box, I shall smash it, as I smash this lamp – look—' He turned his blue glare on a dimly burning lamp, extended a long finger, and the lamp exploded with a little puff, leaving nothing but a spoonful of oily ashes. 'And I'll probably smash you too.'

Michael saw that tears were streaming down his face, and began to feel sorry for him. After all, it must be very disagreeable, if you have worked on something for fifty years, to face even the possibility that someone else may solve it before you.

'Fifty years is a long time,' he said thoughtfully. 'Have you done nothing but work on combinations for the whole of that time? I should think it was terribly boring. Didn't you ever want to do research on anything else? It seems such a waste of your talent. After all, anyone can twiddle a dial.'

He was not sure if this speech was very well phrased, but it seemed to go down all right.

'You are a young man of astounding impertinence,' Borlock said slowly. 'It is true that at times during the fifty years I grew very nearly mad with boredom. It is also true that I should have preferred to do research into the structure and source of light. But down in this black hole the facilities for research of that kind are limited.'

'But you are a magician,' said Michael, puzzled, 'you're frightfully wise and powerful, anyone can see that. Why did you stay here? I'm sure with all your magic you could have got away.'

'Of course I could,' said Borlock angrily. 'Perhaps it doesn't occur to you, you little Palace-bred brat, that I was given this box in trust; the task was assigned to me as the Underworld's wisest man. Heaven knows I disapprove entirely of this invasion plan, but it would have been a violation of that trust to escape and leave the task unfinished. But when it is finished – ah!' he sighed, 'How gladly will I leave this race of ignoble Under Beings and live with some kindly nation in the light of the sun. I have never felt at one with the aims of the people in Down

Under; sometimes I suspect that I come of a different race.'

Borlock seemed calmer now, perhaps more open to argument. Michael felt that the most important thing was to solve the secret of what the box could do before the old man destroyed it in a fit of rage.

Glancing at the box, Michael was convinced that if only he could get his finger on the dial he would know the right word to open it. And when it was open – then it would be time enough to worry about the next step. Obviously he would have to get it to Astalon to help save the Kingdom. It could not be left here as another weapon for the Under People.

It was still necessary to be diplomatic, though.

'Borlock,' he said cautiously, 'I hate to bother you, but I've had no food for days and I feel rather faint. I wonder if I could have something to eat?'

Borlock looked at him pityingly. 'These Earth Children,' he murmured. 'No stamina, no stamina at all. He's young, though. State your needs, child.' He made a couple of passes with his hand.

Later in life when Michael remembered this occasion he was sorry that he had missed the opportunity to have roast peacock or some such rare and out of the ordinary delicacy, but at the time he could think of nothing but the simplest food.

'Might I have some biscuits?' he said modestly.

The old man nodded. 'Biscuits,' he repeated, sketching an invisible hatch.

'And perhaps a cup of tea?' said Michael, encouraged. 'Won't you join me?'

'Pot of tea,' Borlock called down the hatch. 'For two.' In a moment the tea and biscuits appeared on a battered green tin tray. Michael poured out two cups from the fat brown pot and added milk and sugar. He handed Borlock his with a biscuit in the saucer, and the magician and the boy sat down opposite each other, feeling oddly formal.

After the first nibble of biscuit and sip of delicious hot, sweet tea, Michael began,

'Will they give you a reward when you find out the secret of the box?'

'No, child. I don't work for reward,' Borlock replied, stirring his tea meditatively.

'Not even a medal or a decoration?'

'They don't have things like that down here,' said the old man with a dry sniff.

'So there's really nothing personal about the discovery?'

'Not in the way of fame or glory, no. But I should know that I had done it.'

'Well, look,' Michael proceeded slowly. 'You're a scientist. Scientists work together in teams, don't they? They believe it doesn't matter who discovers something, so long as everybody helps and the thing is discovered?

'I should think you must have tried every single word that the combination could be, but isn't. Now *I* know a word which would fit, and which you probably haven't tried, and I have a sort of feeling that it is the right word. I don't know why, but I have. Supposing I tried it, and it worked, it would be just as much a result of all you've done as what I did, because if you hadn't ruled out all those words, I'd probably never have thought of this one.'

He gulped down some tea, fixing anxious eyes on Borlock's face.

Borlock sighed. The tea and biscuits were plainly having a mollifying effect on him. The blue was fading off his face and hands, and he looked again like a harassed, worried old man, and not a vengeful Necromancer.

'I daresay you're right,' he said at length. 'And if you think you have the right word I suppose I can't resist letting you try it. Anyhow, perhaps it will be wrong,' he added hopefully.

'If it is right,' said Michael, trying to keep his eagerness down, 'you can have all the credit, I promise, because I'm not a bit interested in that.'

'No, boy, no,' the old man said, sighing again. 'It's kind of you, but that wouldn't be just, and it wouldn't make any difference.'

Michael ate his last biscuit, wondering how to broach the second half of his plan, but while he was still thinking, Borlock rose.

'Come along then, child, stop munching and let us see,' he said rather mournfully, 'whether you have successfully pitted your tiny wits against the problem which has defeated Borlock.' With a hand on Michael's shoulder he propelled him forward.

Throughout the meal Michael had taken the precaution of holding the magic staff, and he now slipped it into his pocket. Arrived at the table, Borlock watched Michael, looking sardonic, and also sad.

Michael examined the box closely for the first time and then unhesitatingly dialled 'M-I-C-K-L-E'.

There was a whirring, grinding noise from inside the box. Michael forgot his dignity and clutched Borlock's hand.

'Listen!' he cried. 'It's working!'

The box was shaking with the violence of the processes taking place inside it. There was a violent crackling. The lid sprang open, and a beam of such blinding, dazzling brilliance shone out that Michael instinctively slammed it down again.

'We've done it!' he shouted to Borlock. 'We've opened it!'

Borlock was speechless, but he seized Michael's hand and waved it to and fro. He was weeping with happiness.

'Oh, what a relief,' he cried. 'I didn't realize how much it had been weighing on me all these years. Now I don't care who did it or what's in it – I can get on with something else!'

Michael pounced on this opportunity. 'In that case you won't mind—'

But at that moment there was a heavy banging on the outer door, which burst open. Footsteps clattered down the passage and the leader of the guard came in.

'Time's up!' he said. 'Midnight's passed and U-day's begun. Come on, Borlock, you're wanted for consultation at the camp. Bring the captive – we'll want him for bargaining. Never mind the dratted box, chuck it in the river, I should.'

'But it's open!' cried Borlock. 'It's just this minute come open.'

'Oh, well, so much the better. Bring it along then. Leave the boy under your spell, that'll save trouble. We can carry him out.' He called in two more guards.

Luckily through this short conversation Michael had been standing stock still as if paralyzed, and he now made himself as stiff as possible. The men picked him up by his elbows and armpits and carried him to a truck which was waiting outside. It was drawn by two of the giant worms.

Michael was tortured by the desire to look round and see if Borlock was following with the box. Mercifully after a moment he heard the old man's voice asking one of the guard to shut his front door as his hands were full. Borlock and some of the men climbed into the back with Michael, two others jumped up in front, cracking whips, and they were off, rattling over the rocky ground.

16

That fine morning Mickle was pleased to see, from his post in the walnut tree, that the Kingdom of Astalon was rapidly mobilizing for war. Unfortunately, since it was more than four hundred years since the last war, most of the equipment was sadly out of date. The cavalry had some blunt spears, while the artillery was equipped only with crossbows and muzzle-loading guns. There were a few giant catapults, and one aircraft: a balloon, which had been inflated with gas and was now bobbing about in the Palace garden, straining on its cords which were tied to the sundial. There were also two fog-throwers.

The King was having terrible difficulties. The General Staff frankly thought he was mad, for none of them believed in magic, and they were not inclined to mobilize the army on the word of a cat, a horse, a bat, some rooks, and a child's message. How were they to know that the whole thing was not a hoax?

Nevertheless the King, backed up by the Queen, had finally prevailed on them.

'Let's go over to Dingle Warren,' Mickle presently said to Minerva, 'and see how things are going.'

Among the streams of cavalry and infantry moving in that direction, a cat and a horse riding in the little red truck provided by the magic collar were not particularly noticeable. They were able to find a quiet spot near the top of a bracken-covered hillside, near the fog-throwers. Both animals were anxious. Minerva hated violence, and Mickle was constantly worrying about the Prince.

They could see the whole area from their point of vantage. Minerva looked superciliously at some of the cavalry horses and said that they would be better employed pulling farm carts – which, in fact, they had been doing until recently.

'Look, look!' exclaimed Mickle, suddenly interrupting her.

As they watched, the slope facing them shook, heaved, and began to move. Slowly dark cracks appeared running straight up and down the hill, widened until they were huge gashes, and then with a thunderous roar the whole hillside opened outwards like a trapdoor and fell on the bottom of the valley. The air was full of dust and smoke for several minutes, but even so it was possible to distinguish a huge square opening leading back into the hill. Out of this opening without a second's delay large black airborne things began to pour in a solid, well-ordered formation. They buzzed and zoomed, and were about the size of elephants.

'Good heavens,' said Mickle, 'what are those? One balloon won't be much use against that lot.'

Minerva began weeping, but Mickle watched attentively.

'Look, Minerva,' he said, 'dry your eyes with your forelock. This is interesting.'

Minerva obediently mopped her eyes. She was longer-sighted than Mickle – in any case a horse sees objects magnified about eight times larger than a cat does – and after a moment she exclaimed,

'Why, they're ants!'

'Ants,' Mickle agreed grimly. 'Flying ants. See what they're doing.'

They were flying very low, regardless of the crossbow and catapult-bolts aimed at them, and spraying out something white.

'What can it be for?' said Minerva, puzzled.

But Mickle exclaimed, 'Look what it's doing to our army!'

The men nearest them, part of a crack cavalry regiment, had been waiting, ready mounted, for the command to charge. When the white jet from the flying ants blew over them they sat dazed for a moment and then began, one by one, to topple off their horses like sacks. The horses did not seem to be affected.

'They're not all dead?' said Minerva in horror.

'No, they're not,' said Mickle, studying the man beside him. 'It's a sort of paralysis so far as I can see. They're not even unconscious.' To prove this he stuck his claws into the sergeant of the troop, who darted a furious glance at him but could not move a finger. 'I wonder if the effect is lasting?'

'But this is terrible,' cried Minerva, 'they're flying all over the country. There won't be a man left to fight.'

This was only too true. The Under Ant Force was making a systematic tour of the Kingdom, spraying every square mile. When the process was complete, the black ants returned to their base at Dingle Warren, two more slabs of hillside opened, and out of the entrances thus formed poured an orderly mass of Under-soldiers, riding giant worms, followed by trucks, drawn by more giant worms. A camp was established, and by dusk all the Under Forces were on foreign soil.

'Let's creep up to their camp and see if we can pick up some information,' Mickle said.

All the Under-troops were being addressed by their commander – in whom Mickle recognized the man who had questioned him.

'We have done excellently so far,' he was saying, 'thanks to our heroic Ant Force. Every Astalon citizen is paralyzed for seventy-two hours. All the inhabitants must now be disarmed. The Royal Family, and any citizens of importance, must be dissolved. Now disperse.'

At this moment Mickle heard a hoarse panting in his ear. He looked round and saw Lord Porty.

'Caw!' said the rook, 'you haven't half led me a dance. Been looking for you everywhere. That Bat's been back. He asked me to give you a message from His Nibs. He's got the box, and he's coming as fast as he can, but you're to warn his family because they're in great danger. Okay?'

'He needn't have told me about his family,' said Mickle, 'I know. It's excellent about the box. Thanks very much.'

'Roger,' said the rook. 'Quite a picnic here, eh? Paw lookout for our side. Ants the size of crocodiles – caw blimey!'

By this time the sun was setting. When Mickle turned back to Minerva he found her, to his great surprise, talking to a monkey. Mickle had never been on social terms with monkeys, and approached with suspicion; but the occasion was too urgent for formality. 'Minerva,' he said. 'Somehow we've got to delay the Under Forces; prevent them getting to the Palace.'

'Ah,' she said, 'perhaps our young friend here can help. He's the mascot of the Fog Throwing Corps; his patron, the sergeant, is under the weather just now.'

'Can you fire a fog-thrower?' said Mickle hopefully. 'That's exactly what we want.'

Minerva cantered with the monkey to where the fog-throwers stood abandoned.

'Now,' said Mickle. 'Raise a nice pea-souper, can you?'

The monkey clambered learnedly about among the controls while Mickle and Minerva watched with close attention.

'I think I could do that,' said Mickle, after he had watched for a little, and a thin stream of fog was beginning to spurt from the nozzle of the monkey's projector, which was fed by a moving band of capsules.

Mickle moved to the other machine and began hooking out levers with his paw and twirling dials, repeating the monkey's actions with careful precision. This strenuous work dislodged the ruby sceptre-stone, which he had been carrying tucked under his collar, and it fell on to the band of capsules and vanished into the loading carriage before he could rescue it.

'Bother,' he said, 'I hope it doesn't wreck the machine. Is any fog coming out yet, Minerva?'

She had taken two steps towards the nozzle when the machine began to rock, and with a high humming roar a white-hot, shining projectile burst out of it and hurtled in the direction of the Under-Camp. Two seconds later they saw the whole piece of land on which the flying ants were grounded lift and disintegrate. Then the bank of fog which had been piling up rolled down, and engulfed the scene.

'Dear me,' said Mickle, 'how unexpected. That's done for those ants, anyway. I suppose it must have been the ruby; the Queen did say it was a stone of power.'

'*You* said it would be safer in your hands than the King's,' remarked Minerva drily.

They left the monkey still making fog and went down to the Under-Camp to reconnoitre.

'That's odd,' said Minerva, sniffing, 'I can smell water.' She peered ahead into the fog.

'Go carefully,' advised Mickle, also sniffing. Suddenly Minerva flung back on her haunches with a violent whinny. A steep cliff dropped away in front of them. Far below at the foot of it they could dimly see water lapping.

'Gracious,' said Mickle, 'the explosion must have blasted this out. But what a depth! Let's work along it and see what's happened to the camp.'

The Under-Camp was now a scene of wild confusion. Nearly all the worm-trucks, the loaded worms, and the fighting ants had been lost.

The Black Commander was addressing the troops once more.

'Men!' he said in a voice like a trumpet blast. 'I have to tell you of a disaster to our nation. Due to some devilish weapon used by the enemy, not only have we lost most of our weapons and vehicles, but also our beloved city, Down Under, is no more.'

A bitter groan came from the Under soldiers assembled round him.

'Luckily there was little loss of life, for all our patriotic citizens are here, but reports from the last worm-trucks to leave inform me that the cave roof has been wrecked by the explosion, surface water has flowed in, and our cherished home has been flooded. This black lake to the south is all that is left of Down Under. The Kingdom of Astalon is now vitally necessary to us, since our own homeland has been destroyed. On with the invasion! We march at once!'

There was a roar of assent at the end of his words, and the Under Army dispersed into the fog in search of transport.

'Here, I'm off before somebody catches me,' said Minerva. 'What about you, Mickle?'

But Mickle was thinking of the flooded city, and wondering where Michael could be.

17

As the worm-truck gathered speed the leader of the guard turned to Borlock and said,

'Have you really got that box open at last?'

'Yes,' Borlock answered.

'Let's have a look inside.'

'I don't know if you ought,' said the sage doubtfully. 'I haven't had time to test it yet.'

'Oh, come on. It can't bite us.'

Michael watched anxiously. Borlock steadied himself against the side of the truck and dialled M-I-C-K-L-E as he had seen Michael do. The lid sprang open more easily this time, letting out the dazzling beam of light. Michael struggled to keep his eyes on the inside of the box, and presently saw that it was lined with red velvet and contained a diamond as big as an orange which was giving out the ray. After a moment his eyes ceased to stream; a feeling of confidence and happiness grew in him, and for the first time he was certain that his Kingdom would be successful in the war.

He turned to look at the others. Borlock seemed to be drawing knowledge and power out of the diamond with his eyes. But the guards—

'Borlock, look – look what's happening to them,' Michael cried.

Their eyes were goggling, their mouths were open, their hair was vanishing, their skin was turning scaly, they were shrinking.

'They are turning into fish,' said Borlock serenely. 'It was to be expected. Call the driver.'

'Hey!' Michael called. The truck slowed and stopped, the driver and his companion turned – and the same change overtook them. The worms which were pulling the truck also shrank, and resumed the size proper to normal earthworms.

'We should put the fish into water,' said Borlock after a pause. 'We are not far from the river here.' He collected the gasping flapping creatures in his cloak and strode off with them.

'Do not look at the ray for too long,' he warned when he came back.

'But what is the ray?' said Michael, shutting the lid. 'Why has it turned them to fish?'

'It is one of the Diamonds of Eden. There have been only three or four others in the history of the world. King Solomon had one, another was said to be in the possession of Prester John.'

'But what is their power? What do they do?'

'What its full powers are, no one can say,' answered Borlock, 'though I hope to have an opportunity to study this one. But one of its powers, as you see, is that of making bodies take on their true form.'

'But were those men really fish?'

'Evidently,' said Borlock. 'Indeed, I had long suspected it. Their dark, damp, unjoyous life in the cave, always working for an ignoble end, had reduced the man-element and left the fish-element in the ascendant.'

'But what about us? Why didn't we change into something else?'

'In your case, I suppose,' replied Borlock with a half smile, 'it is because the human-boy element in you is the main one. Though you will find yourself somewhat changed.'

Michael glanced down at himself curiously, but could see no difference.

'As for myself – I have always been a philosopher, concerned with the pursuit of knowledge, my store of which has been increased a hundredfold by the Diamond. That is why I am able to tell you about it. It emits the ray of truth.'

There was a moment's silence.

'Well, let's get on,' exclaimed Michael, 'let's go and shine it on all the Under-People who are invading Astalon, and turn them all into fish before they do any harm.'

'An excellent suggestion. But how shall we proceed without worm-traction?'

'I know,' said Michael. 'We'll have to keep the box shut, though.'

He put two fingers in his mouth, whistled piercingly, and called, 'Glob! Glob! Glob!' Then listened.

Presently they heard a kind of walloping rustle, and the grateful Glob arrived at a worm-gallop.

'I was with a reserve detachment,' the worm panted, 'but I threw my rider when I heard your whistle. What can I do for you, kind friend?'

'Can you carry us to the surface?'

'Enchanted to render worm-aid,' said Glob, and stood for them to mount.

At this moment Michael felt a light tap on his cheek, and, turning round, saw the little bat, who carefully unrolled a hair from his claw and gave it to him.

'It's one of Minerva's,' he explained. 'The King and Queen have your message. Your cat friend was there, too.'

'Oh, I *am* grateful to you,' exclaimed Michael fervently. 'Can I take any more messages?'

'Yes, please! Fly to Mickle and tell him that my family are

in dreadful danger. And tell him I've got the box. Can you do that?'

'Certainly,' said the bat, and flitted off once more.

'There is need for haste,' said Borlock, mounting behind Michael. 'Wyburn intends to dissolve your family as soon as the country is occupied.'

Glob began to move, slowly at first, then slipping over the ground in a kind of racing wriggle. Michael, used to horseback riding, found himself at a disadvantage, but Borlock sat the worm to perfection, leaning back slightly and swaying to its ripple. The rock walls flashed by on either side, and Michael estimated that they must have been doing at least forty miles an hour. His main difficulty was in keeping his feet from scraping the floor, without overbalancing.

'Who is Wyburn?' he asked presently. 'And what does "dissolve" mean?'

'He is the Commander, Roger Wyburn, grandson of the Roger Wyburn who stole the treasure.'

'Oh, goodness, the treasure!' exclaimed Michael. 'I meant to find that too. Still the box is the most important thing, and we must get to my family; we'll have to come back for the treasure. I hope you'll come and live in our kingdom now.' He had taken a great liking to Borlock since the diamond had been opened. 'We could find you a tower, or an observatory, or whatever you like to work in, and you could advise my father – he's always getting into muddles – and study the diamond, and teach me . . . '

They had been streaking up a spiral ramp, which ran round the walls of Down Under. Now Glob stopped for a breather.

'I do hope we're going the right way,' said Michael. 'What do you think has been happening up there?'

Borlock explained about the flying ants and the paralysis spray. 'In a concentrated form – such as is to be used on your family – it dissolves people entirely.'

Michael leapt on to Glob's back again. 'Please let's go on!'

At that moment a loud rumbling began, which became more and more deafening. Then Borlock pointed upwards – he could not possibly have made himself heard – and Michael, following the direction of his finger, saw a v-shaped crack of light wriggle across the cave roof. It widened with startling speed and light flooded the cave. Not only light – tons and tons of water and rock came crashing through the huge gap as the roof widened and crumbled. Before their eyes the city of Down Under melted and vanished under the flood.

Borlock tapped Michael's shoulder and made urgent signals to start. The gallant Glob needed no urging and they were off with a jerk, hurtling up the steep tunnel, with water rising behind them. In twenty minutes they saw a light ahead, which increased until they reached one of the huge entrances blasted for the invasion. Here Glob had to slow down across an expanse of broken rock, which was hard on his stomach, and instantly two men in the Under-uniform barred the way with flags.

'Stop!' they shouted. 'All transport is requisitioned for officers.'

One of the men recognized Michael.

'It's the Upstairs boy – the prisoner – he must have escaped. Grab him!'

'Quick, open the box,' Michael muttered to Borlock.

The lid shot open rapidly this time. Borlock raised the box so that the ray shone into the foggy dusk. Two men vanished, and only the noise of flapping and gasping on the ground showed that the ray had done its work. Unfortunately Glob had vanished too; a finger-length earthworm mournfully waved his front end at them and vanished under a stone.

There was nothing they could do but trudge on. Presently they heard a confused noise of shouts and the whinnying of horses. The fog began to resolve into a mass of struggling figures, men and horses all mixed up.

All of a sudden a joyful neigh in Michael's ear made him jump.

'Michael! Thank heaven you're back!' Turning, he looked into the affectionate face of Minerva. He hugged her.

'How wonderful to run into you. What's going on?'

'No time to tell you much,' she said. 'You must get to the Palace right away. These are my friends from the cavalry delaying the Under Army's advance on the Palace. Quick, jump on my back. Or – no, I'm a bit winded. I'll ask these fellows to take you on.'

'This is Borlock, who is helping me,' Michael said. 'Can one of them carry him?'

Minerva let out a shrill whinny. 'Oh gosh,' she muttered, as a group of chargers came cantering up, 'it would be *this* lot.'

The chargers stared haughtily down their Arab noses at the shabby old mare.

'Beg y' pawdon?' one of them said. 'You speakin' to us, my good person? Dontchew know that we are the Bloods – the cream of the crack corps of the smartest cavalry regiment in Astalon? Kindly don't presume.'

'Yes, I know, I know,' snapped Minerva. 'And I wouldn't speak to you blue-blooded bone-headed boobies if it wasn't life and death. This is Prince Michael and he wants to be taken to the Palace double-quick.'

'Oh, of ca-horse, of ca-horse,' the leader said, blushing strawberry roan. 'Didn't recognize your Highness in the fog.'

The change was made. 'I'll follow you,' Minerva called. 'You'll find Mickle at the Palace. Now gallop, you oat-fed oafs!'

In a thunder of hoofs they raced off into the fog, only

pausing at intervals of five miles for Michael and Borlock to change to fresh mounts.

'I hope we're on the right road,' said Michael peering ahead.

At the Palace an advance party had arrived. They were disarming all the unconscious inmates, and had put the King and Queen and two Field-Marshals into the Throne Room, ready for dissolution as soon as the Commander should arrive.

Michael and Borlock arrived with their posse of chargers and dismounted in the orchard, which was deserted.

Michael led Borlock, by hedge and shrubbery, up to his bedroom window. He rightly guessed that to try and enter the Palace by a door would be to court trouble.

His bedroom was a scene of wreckage, as if it had been hastily searched.

'Open the ray,' Michael whispered. The great beam shone down the stairway ahead of them, making the chandeliers look like clusters of pale coins. They stole across to the doorway of the Throne Room. Borlock lifted the diamond in its box and held it on high.

An astonishing scene began, as the Under People shrank and wilted into fish, while the inert members of the King's household began, in most cases, to stir and stretch and come to themselves. There were some exceptions. The Prime

Minister of Astalon gave an extraordinary bleat, and galloped from the room on all fours, growing wool visibly as he went; the Chief of Staff was replaced by a faithful but stupid-looking bulldog.

Michael was so fascinated that he forgot for a moment to see if his parents were there, until he heard his mother's voice, full of joy and relief, calling his name. Then he ran forward and hugged them. 'Thank goodness we got here in time!' he cried.

The greeting they gave him was warm and loving.

'How you've grown – and how handsome you are,' his mother kept exclaiming.

Michael glanced at himself in the Throne Room mirror and did notice that he seemed to have grown a foot, and looked, somehow, different and more grown up, but he had too much on his mind to pay his changed appearance more than passing attention. There was so much to tell them, about the Under People and Borlock and the ray.

'Now it only remains,' said Borlock, 'to work the change on the rest of the Under-forces—'

A sudden hush fell. Turning his head, Michael saw the cause.

Roger Wyburn, the Commander, had arrived and was striding towards them. His face was white, his eyes blazing. Borlock turned the ray on him, but it had no apparent effect. He came up to the wise man, hissed at him the single word 'Traitor!' snatched the box, and knocked him spinning with a brutal blow. Then he turned and was out of the room in a flash. Everyone seemed stunned except Michael, who tore in pursuit after a frantic glance at Borlock's motionless body.

Through the entrance hall he chased Wyburn, took the front steps in bounds, six at a time, and followed him round into the Palace garden. Then he saw what Wyburn was making for – the captive balloon, straining at its guy-ropes in the rose garden. Just as Wyburn reached it, something black launched itself like a cannon ball at his head and clung to him.

Michael shouted, '*Mickle!*' and ran on, his heart pounding.

Wyburn was clawing frantically with his arms, trying to dislodge Mickle, who stuck like a burr. Then Michael saw with a sick sensation that he had pulled a dagger from its sheath.

'Come a step nearer and I'll chop the cat's head off,' he said savagely.

Michael felt in his pockets for a weapon and found nothing but a wooden stick. What could it be? Then he remembered Borlock's staff.

He drew it out, exerting all his will.

'By the power in this staff I charge you to drop the thing in your hands,' he gasped.

Wyburn gave a satirical smile; then it changed to one

of incredulity. He looked at his hands, which had become stiff and nerveless. With a clatter, the dagger and box fell to the ground. Michael dropped the staff to grab the box, and in that moment Wyburn struck Mickle off his shoulder and flung himself into the balloon, yanking the guy-ropes from their moorings bodily. He leaned out to shout down,

'You've won this time, but don't think it's for good! I'll be back to settle accounts with you!' Then the balloon soared into the dark and was gone.

'Pity we didn't get him,' said Mickle, putting his whiskers to rights. 'But at least you have the ray.'

Michael took the ray and staff, and went back to see what had become of Borlock. When he reached the Throne Room he found himself overwhelmed with a terrible weariness. He saw with relief that Borlock had recovered and was lying on a sofa being given something to drink by the Queen. Michael handed him the box, searching his exhausted mind for words.

'Borlock,' he stammered, 'tell them how it works – turn the others into fish—'

Borlock's intelligent nod was the last thing he saw before darkness rushed over him.

18

Michael came to himself in his own bed, and lay in puzzled contentment for several minutes wondering where he was. Then his memory began to come back. He remembered Borlock, the escape with Glob, and the flood that overwhelmed Down Under.

'The treasure!' he exclaimed suddenly.

A bump in the bed below his knees rose up and revealed itself as Mickle.

'What about the treasure?' he asked.

'It's lost again,' Michael told him, and explained about the flooded city.

'I thought something like that must have happened,' said Mickle, and he recounted all that he and Minerva had been doing while the Prince was underground. For an hour the two of them took it in turns telling their stories and fitting in the bits.

'It's a pity about the treasure, all the same,' Michael said regretfully. 'We ought to dive for it sometime. Still, it's better to have the ray. We don't know all it can do yet.'

Mickle began to laugh silently. 'We do know one thing it can do,' he said. 'In the course of transforming all the Under-men into fish (which has now been done; they were at it all night) it has turned quite a number of your father's subjects into animals and some into stones and logs of wood. Miss Simkin turned into a lizard. I daresay they could be spared if that was their real nature.'

'What have they done with all the fish?'

'Dumped them in the new lake – fishing prohibited.'

A footman brought in breakfast on a tray and Michael ate ravenously.

'Where's Borlock?' he asked presently.

'In the V.I.P. guest room, being looked after by the Palace doctor. He had a nasty knock but he's all right.'

'And Wyburn?'

'Not a trace of him or the balloon – he's completely escaped. I'm afraid you may have trouble with him later because he's evidently a real man and not a fish.'

'I must get up and see everybody,' said Michael, struggling out from under the tray.

He went to the chief guest chamber in search of Borlock. As he approached the door he heard voices, and he found the King and Queen talking to Borlock, who was dressed, but lying on a sofa.

'He's a good boy,' the King was saying. 'I hope it won't be too hard on him. Ah, my dear boy, we were just speaking of you.'

'The learned Borlock has promised to make his home with us,' the King went on, looking trustingly at Borlock, 'and in these lucky circumstances I am going to do an unconventional thing.'

Michael gazed at him attentively.

'After all these anxieties and excitements I find, I confess it, that I am too old and tired to go on ruling.' The King passed his hand over his brow, and the Queen took his hand and patted it protectively. 'I am going to abdicate so that you can rule, my son. You are young, but you have shown yourself to be capable in the recent crisis, and if you are helped by Borlock I am sure you will do well.'

'But Father,' said Michael, stunned by the unexpectedness of all this, 'you're not old.'

'I feel old,' replied the King, simply. 'I find that all I want to do is to collect seashells. You will rule much better, I am sure.'

Borlock gave Michael an encouraging nod.

'You will find ruling no hardship, I promise you. The diamond has done more for you than you yet realize. You are not a boy any longer.'

'It's so sudden,' Michael said. 'May I go away and think about it?'

They watched him affectionately as he left the room.

He went into the garden, which was silent and full of hazy October sunshine. Walking slowly across the leaf-strewn lawns he found Mickle sitting in his special flowerbed.

'Hullo,' said Mickle, noticing his dragging gait, 'have they put you on the throne?'

'Yes,' said Michael. 'Did you know?'

'No, but I expected it. Cheer up. It won't be as bad as you think. Borlock will help you. He's a sensible man; we had a talk last night. Now, let's go and see Minerva.'

They had just reached Minerva when Michael noticed two cats galloping diagonally so as to cut them off. One was Blackie from the Home Farm; one, a tabby, that Michael had not seen before.

'Mickle!' Blackie panted, 'Sorry to bother you – urgent message.'

'Well, what?' Mickle said impatiently. 'Who from?'

'Speak up, Stripes,' muttered Blackie. The tabby, a shy, wild-looking cat, plucked up his courage and recited, all in a rush, without pausing for breath:

'I live in the woods behind the Home Farm and this morning I was up in the big hollow oak tree when looking down I saw passing through it a cats' funeral with a hundred cats all in black, four in the lead carrying a coffin draped in a purple cloak, and on the coffin there stood a small golden crown.'

Mickle had listened at first without paying much

attention, but at the last words his eyes grew rounder and rounder, until, when Stripes finished, he let out a deep breath, and exclaimed,

'My stars, old Peter's dead, and I'm the King of the Cats!'

'Mickle!' the Prince exclaimed, 'What *do* you mean?'

'Oh, I knew it was bound to come some day,' Mickle said crossly, 'I think you gathered on All Cats' Night that I was next in line to the Cat throne, but I thought old Peter was good for another seven or eight lives yet. *What* a nuisance: pomp – formality – stately manners – having to be a reigning cat all the time—'

'Cheer up,' said Michael with friendly malice, 'it won't be as bad as you think.'

'I suppose I'll have to go and be received,' Mickle sighed. He hurried off importantly, Blackie and Stripes respectfully in attendance.

'But – when shall I see you again?' Michael called, feeling rather desolate. Were all his friends going to leave him?

'Oh, soon – very soon,' Mickle called back, waving his tail. 'You come to my coronation, I'll come to yours.' He disappeared into the wood.

Minerva chuckled. 'Kings here, kings there,' she said. 'I suppose I shall have to pay to speak to you soon.'

'You won't go away, Minerva, will you?' Michael said, throwing his arms round her old brown neck. 'You won't leave me too?'

'Not unless they decide to make me Queen of the old Crocks and Hacks,' she said. 'Come, come, your Majesty, don't be downhearted. There's good times coming. Nicodemus and Brock send their love and ask you to visit them as soon as you can spare the time. Now you'd better go back to the Palace. Chin up!'

So Michael grinned at her and straightened his shoulders, and turned to go back to the Palace where his friends were waiting for him.

AN EPISODE OF SPARROWS

Rumer Godden

'A masterpiece of construction and utterly,
realistically convincing ... Lovejoy, Tip and Sparkey
were so real to me that they have stayed alive in my
head for more than fifty years' Jacqueline Wilson

Someone has been digging up the private garden in the Square.
Miss Angela Chesney of the Garden Committee is sure that
a gang of local boys is to blame, but her sister, Olivia, isn't so
certain. She wonders why the neighbourhood children –
'sparrows', she calls them – have to be locked out: don't
they have a right to enjoy the garden too?

Nobody has any idea what sends Lovejoy Mason
and her few friends in search of 'good garden earth'. Still
less do they imagine where their investigation will lead them –
to a struggling restaurant, a bombed-out church and,
at the heart of it all, a hidden garden.

THE SERIAL GARDEN

Joan Aiken

'Joan Aiken's invention seemed
inexhaustible, her high spirits a blessing, her
sheer storytelling zest a phenomenon. She was
a literary treasure' Philip Pullman

'I wish we'll have two children called Mark and Harriet.
And I hope lots of interesting and unusual things will happen
to them. It would be nice if they had a fairy godmother, for
instance. And a phoenix or something out of the ordinary for a
pet. We could have a special day for interesting and unusual
things to happen – say, Mondays. But not always Mondays, and
not only Mondays, or that would get a bit dull'

As a result of their mother's honeymoon wish, Mark
and Harriet Armitage have a fairy godmother, a pet unicorn,
and are prepared for anything life throws at them (especially,
but not always, on a Monday): hatching griffins in the airing
cupboard, Latin lessons with a ghost, furious Furies on the
doorstep, and an enchanted garden locked inside a cereal
packet. Life with the Armitages can be magical, funny,
terrifying – but never, ever dull.

'She was a consummate story-teller,
one that each generation discovers anew'
Amanda Craig, *The Times*

virago

To buy any of our books and to find out more
about Virago Press and Virago Modern Classics,
our authors and titles, as well as events and
book club forum, visit our websites

www.virago.co.uk
www.littlebrown.co.uk

and follow us on Twitter

@ViragoBooks

To order any Virago titles p & p free in the UK,
please contact our mail order supplier on:

+ 44 (0)1832 737525

Customers not based in the UK should contact
the same number for appropriate postage
and packing costs.